By ASHLYN KANE

American Love Songs
With Claudia Mayrant & CJ Burke: Babe in the Woodshop
A Good Vintage
Hang a Shining Star

With Morgan James
Hair of the Dog
Hard Feelings
Return to Sender
Winging It

With Bethany Brown
LOST BOYS AND LOVE LETTERS SERIES
True North
Picture Perfect
Wild Angels
Broken Wings

Published by DREAMSPINNER PRESS
www.dreamspinnerpress.com

By CLAUDIA MAYRANT

With Ashlyn Kane & CJ Burke: Babe in the Woodshop

Published by DREAMSPINNER PRESS
www.dreamspinnerpress.com

By CJ BURKE

With Ashlyn Kane & Claudia Mayrant: Babe in the Woodshop

Published by DREAMSPINNER PRESS
www.dreamspinnerpress.com

BABE in the WOODSHOP

Ashlyn Kane
& Claudia Mayrant
CJ Burke

DREAMSPINNER PRESS

Published by

DREAMSPINNER PRESS

5032 Capital Circle SW, Suite 2, PMB# 279, Tallahassee, FL 32305-7886 USA
www.dreamspinnerpress.com

This is a work of fiction. Names, characters, places, and incidents either are the product of author imagination or are used fictitiously, and any resemblance to actual persons, living or dead, business establishments, events, or locales is entirely coincidental.

Babe in the Woodshop
© 2016 Ashlyn Kane, Claudia Mayrant & CJ Burke.

Cover Art
© 2016 Alexandria Corza.
http://www.seeingstatic.com
Cover content is for illustrative purposes only and any person depicted on the cover is a model.

ISBN: 978-1-63477-705-6
Digital ISBN: 978-1-63477-706-3
Library of Congress Control Number: 2016907092
Published September 2016
v. 1.0

Printed in the United States of America

∞

This paper meets the requirements of
ANSI/NISO Z39.48-1992 (Permanence of Paper).

CHAPTER ONE

THE GAS gauge on Bellamy Alexander's hand-me-down Chevy Malibu had been broken for years. Sometime between his brother getting married and passing it off to his sister and his sister driving it back to college for her senior year, the gauge gave up the ghost, and no one had told their mother, so it had never gotten fixed. Bell knew that—had known it since he borrowed it from Emily and got stranded during rush hour when he thought he had half a tank. That sort of thing only needed to happen to Bell once to make an impression.

Or so he thought.

When the car sputtered to a halt, he didn't even know what town he was in. He didn't have a map and he hadn't been paying attention. He'd just gotten in his car and pointed it east, and now here he was, somewhere in the foothills of the Appalachians.

More specifically, apparently, he was at Antonio's Pizza—or more accurately in the parking space outside Antonio's Pizza, which sat on a moderately busy street in what otherwise seemed a quiet town. Bell was lucky: he'd been parallel parking, so he didn't have to suffer the indignity of blocking traffic. He simply put the car in neutral, opened his door, and gave it a little shove to coax it the last few inches into the space.

When he turned off the highway, he'd only been thinking about lunch. When he signaled to pull into the parking spot, he was thinking about pizza.

He looked at the Help Wanted sign in the front window and thought his parents didn't believe in fate. "A real man makes his own destiny," Bell's father always said.

Bell didn't see why a real man couldn't take a hint. But first, pizza.

Inside, Antonio's featured a few booths with cracking vinyl, a long, polished bar top starring six beer taps and many a condensation ring, and a smell that reminded Bell he'd only eaten a banana and half a stale granola bar for breakfast. Behind the counter, a woman in her midtwenties was drawing a beer for a fiftysomething guy in a plaid shirt and a trucker hat. The woman smiled at Bell. "Welcome to Antonio's. Have a seat wherever and I'll be right with you!"

Bell figured she was the one to talk to about employment, so he sat at the corner of the bar, a few seats away from any other customer, and scanned the laminated menu taped to the surface. When the woman approached a moment later, she smiled again. "I'm Jenny. What can I get you?"

Bell could play it cool. The past two years had taught him more than he ever wanted to know about playing "the game." But he'd quit because it turned out he hated the rat race, hated the game, hated nineteen-hour workdays and lemon cleanses and bullshit. "I'd like the calzone with mushrooms and peppers, a pint of whatever local brew you have on tap, and the job you have advertised in the window, but I'll settle for the first two."

Jenny studied him for a moment. Bell knew what he looked like. He'd banished his work shirts to the backseat of his car, so he was wearing a ratty polo from his college days, a pair of shorts that could use a wash, and the flip-flops his mother always told him not to drive in. He'd showered in the motel that morning, but he hadn't bothered with gel because he planned to be in the car all day anyway. And he hadn't shaved in a couple of days, not that he had much to shave in the first place. "Let's see your license," Jenny said finally and held out her hand.

Bell dug in his pocket. "You're carding me?" he asked incredulously. He knew he had a baby face, but—

"I'm screening your job application," Jenny said as he handed over his ID. He'd had to renew his license a few years before, so instead of a skinny, pimple-faced teenager, the photo showed him almost as he was—blond, high cheekbones, deep-set blue eyes. In the picture he was pale except for the dark circles, because he'd been up until two working the entire week before. Now, after a few days with real sleep and normal exposure to the sun, he actually had a pretty good tan. "The job's for a delivery driver."

2

"Oh." Bell probably should have asked before he said he wanted the job. Well, it was too late to withdraw his interest, but he certainly wasn't going to offer a résumé filled with fancy useless internships and two years as a junior consultant.

"This says you live in Rhode Island," Jenny said and handed his license back. "Hell of a commute."

"I'm new in town," Bell said earnestly, pulling his most sincere good-citizen face.

Apparently not fooled, Jenny snorted. "I bet you are." Then she shook her head. "Job's Monday to Thursday, noon till ten. Might send you home early if it's slow, and it *can* be slow during the week. Weekend shifts as needed, but we have a guy, he has seniority for the busier days. Pay's minimum wage plus tips."

"Wow, you're really selling this," Bell said admiringly. He wondered how many college kids had applied and then run out the door after this spiel.

Jenny grinned a shark's grin. "I hate wasting time."

Bell could respect that. And truth be told, at least for the time being, he needed occupation more than he needed money. "What happened to your last delivery guy? He find a better job?"

"He retired."

"On that salary!" Bell whistled. "How'd he manage it?"

"He was eighty-seven."

Jesus.

Still, Bell needed a reason to stick around someplace or he was going to drive off the edge of the world. "When can I start?"

Jenny skipped the beer and brought him his calzone to go.

BELL'S FIRST delivery was a small pizza with mushrooms, peppers, and Italian sausage. Jenny handed him the keys to the Volkswagen Rabbit parked out back, smirked, and clapped him on the shoulder. "Good luck."

The Rabbit didn't have GPS, so Bell put the warming bag on the front seat and plugged the address into his phone.

Then he frowned, sighed, and got out of the car.

25A Main Street West, read Jenny's precise looping handwriting. Bell looked at the front of Antonio's: 24 Main Street West.

When traffic cleared, he crossed the street.

25 was a two-story building with dusty front windows. A big sign above the door proclaimed it to be the home of Good Wood— or actually Good Wood Furniture, but *furniture* was written in small letters underneath the main legend.

Bell raised his hand to knock and then stopped himself. Did you knock on a business's door to deliver a pizza? He didn't see a sign saying Open, but there wasn't one saying Closed either, so he tried the door. Chimes tinkled when he opened it—real ones, not an automated buzzer. He looked over his shoulder to see a cluster of small, copper-colored bells hanging from a piece of twine over the doorway. It was an oddly homey touch, and as Bell entered the room, he saw it was far from the only one.

Good Wood didn't look anything like the sleek high-end furniture stores near his former office. There wasn't a hint of chrome or shiny lacquer, but not surprisingly, there was a lot of wood. The space was full almost to the point of being cluttered with all kinds of furniture—dining sets with long or round tables and matching chairs, head and footboards for beds, dressers and armoires. Some of the pieces were definitely antiques or at least made to look that way, heavy and ornately carved, but others were smooth and modern-looking, with simple lines and sinuous curves. Bell had never thought much about furniture other than whether it kept his stuff or his ass off the floor, but the pieces were really something.

A flash of movement caught the corner of his eye, so Bell turned around to see. His own reflection stared back at him from a mirror set in a large, ornate frame. He looked ridiculous standing in his slightly grubby clothes, surrounded by custom furniture, holding a pizza box.

Which was what he was doing there. Not gawking, but delivering pizza. Only no one had come out when the bells rang, so there was no one to give the pizza to.

Bell set the box down on the least-cluttered part of the counter— dark wood polished to a gleaming shine—and looked at the curtained doorway behind. He cleared his throat and rapped on the counter a few times, but before he could say anything, he heard a voice from behind the curtain.

"Sorry! Hands are a bit full, but you can leave it on the counter, Fred. Money's under the ashtray."

Bell looked down, and sure enough, a foot or so down the counter was a ceramic ashtray full of odds and ends. Thankfully they didn't include cigarette butts. The corners of a few folded bills stuck out from underneath. Either the guy was really trusting or small-town living was even more different from the city than he thought.

"But what if I'm not Fred?" Bell reached for the bills, but before he could tug them free, he heard a thunk from behind the curtain and then a few coughs. "You okay?"

"Fine," his customer said as he came through the curtain. He was a shade shorter than Bell's six-one and seemed to be mostly yellow, until Bell realized that was sawdust and woodchips. Black plastic glasses framed kind blue eyes, and a set of safety glasses pushed up on his head made his hair stick up everywhere. He wiped his hands with a mostly clean towel as he moved toward the counter. "Sanding makes dust. Where's Fred?"

"I don't know," Bell said, trying not to stare at the guy's forearms. "Jenny took away my beer and gave me the keys to the Rabbit, along with your pizza, delivery of which did not actually involve driving. But all she said was that there was someone who gets priority for weekends. I assume that's Fred."

"Yep. Fred's the young guy. He's in his sixties."

"I think I can beat that," Bell said and held out his hand, wondering if he could ask why someone across the street from a pizza place would bother with delivery. "I'm Bell, by the way. Nice place."

"Chris McGregor—and that's kind of you, but it's a mess and I know it." He shook Bell's hand. He had nice hands, big and warm and calloused. "You up at the college or something? You're new around here if you don't know Fred."

5

ASHLYN KANE, CLAUDIA MAYRANT & CJ BURKE

"Nope, just running away from home. I stopped for lunch and got a job instead." Bell frowned, suddenly sidetracked. "Hey, is Fred why the Rabbit smells like Icy Hot?"

Chris laughed as he leaned against the counter, arms crossed. Bell didn't know whether to look at his laugh lines or the biceps straining the fabric of his purple T-shirt. "Menthol is Fred's signature scent. He's the easiest man to find in town. Nice guy, but I know way more about his back pain than is strictly necessary for a pizza-based relationship."

"I didn't realize pizza delivery had such strict rules."

"Definitely," Chris said. "For example, no comments on the customer's preferred topping combinations, just like tipping with pennies is rude."

"Quarters, though? Helps a guy out with laundry issues, which in turn helps out with not smelling so much like Icy Hot and oregano."

"See, you understand. You'll go a long way in this business, kid." Chris grinned at him, wide and easy. "As you've probably figured out, pizza delivery in this town can be a lifelong career."

"Sounds like it," Bell said after a moment. Wow, he needed to get a grip. Since when was he incapable of carrying on a conversation with a hot guy without lag time?

"You okay?" Chris's brow furrowed.

"Yeah." Bell blinked and shook himself out of his distraction. "It's—you've got sawdust in your beard."

"Oh." Chris reached under the counter and produced another small towel, presumably cleaner than the first, and scrubbed at the short, neatly trimmed reddish hairs. "Occupational hazard, and the source of a lot of sneezing. Better?"

It wasn't exactly unattractive before. "I just wanted to make sure you get the full Antonio's Pizza experience, unmarred by any environmental pollutants."

"Good sell," Chris said. He tapped the pizza box absently. "Glad to see Antonio's is shifting back to its artisan roots. Does your dark, hidden past contain marketing experience?"

"Maybe," Bell said, "but that usually works against me, so I keep my mouth shut about the degree."

"Wise choice."

They smiled at each other, but Bell couldn't figure out what to say next. He'd already embarrassed himself with the sawdust comment, though he thought it was forgivable—the light catching on Chris's beard, mixed with the dark flecks of wood, had interrupted whatever Bell was thinking.

The sharp ring of Chris's phone saved the silence from becoming too awkward.

"Hello?" Chris laughed as a stream of words poured through the receiver. "Yes, he's here. No, he didn't get lost. We were talking about Fred." He held the phone out to Bell. "Your boss wants to talk to you."

Bell took the phone. It was warm from Chris's hand. "Hi, Jenny."

"Come on back, kid. Got a delivery to one of the sorority houses. Good chance for tips, so hurry the hell up."

THE AROMA from the stack of pizzas made Bell look wistfully at his own forlorn calzone in its to-go box, but he thought better of trying to eat and drive. Probably a good call, as the Rabbit began to sputter a bit as he drove up the steep hill to Sorority Row. He really didn't want to hike the rest of the way to the house and show up dripping sweat on Zeta Pi's dinner. That would not lead to a good tip.

When he pulled up to the house, he took a quick look at himself in the Rabbit's rearview. He still looked as sloppy as he had in the mirror at Good Wood. Bell squinted at his reflection. Sloppy, maybe, but not scary. At least he didn't have any obvious zits and his second-day stubble looked charmingly scruffy—he hoped—instead of borderline disreputable.

Bell just wanted to hand over the pizzas so he could eat his calzone on the way back to the pizzeria. But the sorority president, a tall, pretty girl with corn rows and short shorts, seemed eager to chat.

After the first minute, Bell figured out she was flirting. He racked his memory for the name from the delivery slip. "Hey, uh, Mikayla?"

Mikayla smiled and leaned against the doorjamb as though she was expecting a dinner invitation. "Yeah?"

God, Bell hoped this didn't backfire. Though he supposed he could always buy some gas and hit the road again. "Do you like sausage on your pizza?" he asked, in blatant disregard of Chris McGregor's Pizza Delivery Etiquette.

She gave him a strange look and cocked her head to one side. "Yes…?"

"Yeah, me too," Bell said meaningfully and handed her the pizza boxes.

For a few long seconds, Mikayla stared at him, and he was afraid she wasn't going to get it.

Then she laughed and put the boxes down to reach for her wallet. "Well, you can't blame a girl for trying."

Bell earned a good tip *and* got to eat his calzone, so he was calling it a win.

THE REST of the afternoon was slowish. Bell got a couple more deliveries, but mostly he sat in the back of the restaurant and filled out paperwork. While he dotted the i's and crossed the t's, he chatted with Antonio, who said Bell might as well learn to make himself useful in the kitchen if he was going to stick around, since afternoons tended to feature a lull in deliveries. Bell ended up with dough everywhere and a few more stains on his shirt, but he'd learned a skill, so that was okay.

Bell apologized for the mess, but Antonio only laughed at him. "Your mess!" he chuckled. "My son, he grew up in this kitchen, you know? We kept his playpen in the corner, back before health codes were so strict. You want to see a mess in the kitchen?" He grinned. "Let Joey at the sauce. Hopeless. You? You'll learn."

When they finished with the dough and sauce and there was still nothing to deliver, Bell took his break time to amble down the street to the gas station and pick up a can of gas for the Chevy.

At the end of the night, after Jenny finished counting the till, she glanced at his paperwork. "This address is *also* in Rhode Island."

Bell nodded tiredly and knuckled sleep out of the corners of his eyes. Ten-hour days beat nineteen all around the bush, but learning new routines wore him out. "Yeah, and it's not even mine." He'd put down his parents' address out of sheer desperation. He didn't want to admit on his job application that he'd given up his apartment and was essentially homeless. "Is there a good long-stay motel in town? I need to look for a place, but I don't think I'm going to find one tonight."

Jenny looked like she might be about to offer to let him crash on her couch, but then her phone pinged. She picked it up and glanced at it before returning her attention to Bell. "There's a place back up by the college," she said. "I'll give you the address. You'll probably be making more than a few deliveries there, anyway. It's not fancy, but it's close, and they won't extort you."

"Awesome."

"And here," she said as she handed him a pizza box. At first Bell thought she was about to send him on the last run of the night, but then she said, "Dad made the wrong order. Guy asked for no mushrooms. So it's yours if you want it."

As if on cue, Bell's stomach growled. If he weren't careful, this job could be bad for his cholesterol. "The motel doesn't have a gym, by any chance?"

Jenny laughed. "We can keep you on your feet enough to make up for no gym, as long as you don't subsist entirely on mistake pizzas." She scribbled the motel's address on the back of a menu, then counted out a few bills and handed them to Bell. "I'll start cutting you checks in the next pay cycle, but this should cover tonight. See you at noon, unless you wise up and leave town before you get stuck here like everyone else."

"You're local, though."

"Fourth-generation Pinevillian," she said, "through my mom's side. Dad's from away. Came here for college and never left."

"Sounds nice," Bell said. "We moved around a lot for my dad's job. I'm used to the hit-it-and-quit-it school of relocation." The social-ladder relocating stopped the year Bell started high school, when his dad opened his own practice.

"A lot of people get here because of that, but some of them put down roots. Your first delivery tonight, Chris? We all thought he'd escaped. He had some fancy tie-wearing kind of job for a while. But he came back to settle things when his grandfather died, and never left again. No one stays away for long." She shook her head. "I make it sound like a Stephen King novel. But Pineville's a good place to pull off the road for a while, and I'll keep you busy as long as you want to be here. Meanwhile you look like you're about to fall over. Go on and let me lock up behind you."

Bell put the cash she'd given him into his wallet, then picked up the pizza and the menu with the address of the motel. "Thanks for giving me a chance, Jenny."

"You're cute, charming, and capable of making change—pretty much the ideal pizza guy." Jenny followed him to the door. "Now go get some sleep."

The motel Jenny recommended was only a few miles away from Antonio's. It was set back from the road, behind a row of whitewashed truck tires turned into planters, though there was nothing growing in them. It was less the kind of motel Bell was familiar with, and more a collection of ramshackle cottages that needed a paint job. Bell pulled into the circular drive and went through the door marked Office, where an unshaven man in a tank top was watching a cheerful man selling radar fishfinders on a shopping channel.

"Yeah?"

"Um," Bell said, "Jenny from the pizza place said that you might have a room available."

The man sighed but didn't turn away from the television. "Got one cottage left. One bed, kitchenette, if you stay a month it's 10 percent off. Law says I can't tell you not to bring girls over, but no parties, no smoking indoors."

"No problem with any of that," Bell said as he pulled out his wallet. "I guess night-to-night, to start. I should know pretty soon whether I'm staying in town."

"It's your money," the man said, taking the lone set of keys from a pegboard behind the counter and slapping them down next

10

to a pad of registration forms. "Fill that out while I run your card. Blue key's for laundry, silver key's to your cottage. Take a right from where you're parked and it's the third one on the left. Got a blue door and some artsy glass mobile or whatever hanging from the porch. Last tenant was an art major."

"Thanks," Bell said.

"Welcome to fucking Pineville, kid." The man handed Bell his credit card and the receipt and then went back to his fishfinder infomercial.

Bell parked his car in front of his cottage, grabbed his backpack and pizza, and then let himself in. Even before the door was completely open, he could smell the distinctive scent of roach spray and damp.

The cottage was divided into four tiny rooms—a living room with a brown plaid couch; a bedroom with a twin-size bed and a three-drawer dresser; a bathroom with a small shower, in which the sink was so close to the toilet that Bell was afraid he'd pull both off the wall in the night; and a kitchen with a two-burner stove, a small refrigerator, and a table that was attached to the wall with a hinge. The living room and bedroom had green textured carpet, while the bed and bath had cracked vinyl flooring.

It was the most depressing place Bell had ever paid to sleep in—and probably in the top ten for depressing places he *hadn't* paid to sleep in—including that unregistered hostel in Cornwall, but he was exhausted and smelled like tomato sauce. It would do for now.

Bell wore his flip-flops in the shower, used his own towel, and put on a pair of running shorts and a T-shirt. He curled up on the couch and promised himself he'd go sleep in the car if he heard anything skitter across the floor.

CHAPTER TWO

HE DIDN'T set an alarm, but it turned out he didn't need one, because the clang of the dumpster and truck woke him before eight. He blinked in the dimness of the room and squinted when he accidentally turned toward the window, where the curtains gaped just enough to let in a sharp sliver of sunlight. On the upside, the sunshine promised a nice day. On the downside, it only made the little motel cottage look dingier. He really needed to get out of there.

Bell took another shower, mostly so he could steam some of the wrinkles out of a clean pair of khaki shorts and a checked button-down, but a little bit because he felt like some of the motel's scent was sticking to him, and it wasn't an auspicious odor for starting a new day.

As he shaved in front of the mirror, trying to ignore the greenish tinge the fluorescent light gave his skin, Bell thought about the last time he stayed in a hotel and how different it was. That hotel bathroom had included not only a fancy shaving mirror but also a selection of herb-scented products that promised to cleanse, smooth, or soothe everything from his hair to his feet. He had a trouser press instead of a shower rod to hang his clothes over, and when he took the shiny elevator down to the lobby, it was to take advantage of a buffet breakfast that included a station where a guy would make him an egg-white omelet with free-range turkey sausage and organic spinach.

Then he took his omelet, a blueberry bran muffin, and his fresh-squeezed orange juice to the table he shared with four other bright-eyed junior consultants, their training seminar mentor, and a stack of mock client proposals that had to be evaluated and summarized before their eight-o'clock meeting. Bell was so busy and anxious that he managed only one sip of juice that burned like vinegar in his stomach and just a half bite of omelet, but he swallowed four antacid tablets before lunch that day.

All things considered, a protein bar and vending-machine coffee in a dilapidated cottage didn't seem so bad. But Bell really did need something else to eat, and he wanted to get the lay of the land before he had to be at Antonio's.

There wasn't a lot of Pineville, but what there was seemed pleasant enough. He drove around the college a bit, figuring that would be a good place to be familiar with if he was delivering pizza. Most of the campus buildings were well-maintained red brick, and the way they snuggled into a few hills made the setting that much more charming. A little hamlet of restaurants and shops clustered by the main college gate; there seemed to be good enough odds of finding a breakfast spot that Bell decided to explore on foot. He passed a laundromat, the requisite Starbucks, and then, under a yellow awning, there it was. *Sunshine Cafe—Come in for Breakfast All Day*. Bell figured that was as good an invitation to a meal as a new guy in town was going to get.

A sign in the window read *Thursday: all you can eat pancakes. $5*.
Bell went in.

Every college stereotype Bell knew had crowded in for the morning rush: Mikayla and one of her sorority sisters, a table of guys in athletic jackets, a person with a nose ring and purple-and-green hair eating with one hand and texting with the other. At the counter sat an otherwise very attractive man wearing an actual tweed blazer with corduroy elbow patches.

Bell took the free spot next to Professor Stereotype, let the overworked waiter pour him a coffee, and ordered the special with a side of bacon.

"You want blueberry, banana, or chocolate chip to start? Or just plain?"

Bell wanted one of everything.

His server winked. "My kind of order. Coming up."

Maybe Pineville wouldn't be so bad.

A stack of local newspapers sat next to Bell's neighbor. "Are you going to read that?" Bell asked.

Tweedy passed it over. "All yours. You new in town?"

Bell smiled. "How did you know?"

"Owen didn't know your pancake order." He smiled back. Wow. If only he'd lose the tweed. Maybe Pineville was a secret hideaway for attractive men. "Just about everyone has a weakness for pancakes."

"This looks like the place to have 'em." Bell flipped through the *Pineville Daily Courier* until he found the classifieds, on the inside back cover. He folded the paper to look at the meager For Rent listings.

For the most part, the ads were terribly edited. Bell ruled out the one with three roommates and another whose author claimed the apartment boasted "alot of natural light." A third was listed outside his projected budget.

Professor Tweed looked over at the page. "If you're looking for a place, you picked a bad time of year, I'm afraid. The students snatch up most of the apartments by August." He didn't sound smug about that, precisely, but Bell felt like he was being judged for not having a life crisis six to eight weeks sooner.

"I guess so," Bell said a little glumly, not enthused by the prospect of staying in the motel any longer than absolutely necessary. Maybe he could buy something to make it remotely more appealing? Or maybe there was another motel with a lower roach population?

"Actually." Tweedy looked him up and down, clearly assessing. "I've got an apartment for rent, if you're interested. My property manager hasn't listed it yet because our tenant just moved out with no notice. It's not in one of those big fancy communities with pools and tennis courts, but I'm thinking you're not exactly the type."

"No," Bell answered. "Not anymore." He took a deep breath. *Please think I'm at least worth considering.* "Do you have a rental application, or…?"

Professor Tweedy reached into his jacket and pulled out a crinkled notebook. He scribbled down a phone number, tore out the page, and handed it to Bell. "I have to go or I'm going to be late to class, but here's the manager's number if you want to give him a call."

Bell took it. "Thanks."

But Tweedy was already gone, his money tucked under the edge of his plate, and Owen appeared with a plate of pancakes that made

Bell's stomach growl so loud he looked around to see if anyone else had heard.

He ate every last bite.

Then, crossing his fingers, he put the number in his phone and pressed Call.

It rang… and rang… and rang. Bell kept expecting to hit voice mail, but no dice. Finally, on the nineteenth ring, someone picked up. "Good Wood Furniture."

Bell frowned. He hadn't expected a familiar voice. "I, uh, sorry. I was calling about an apartment."

He thought he must have the wrong number, but Chris said, "Not Fred?"

It hadn't been so long since Bell met a cute guy that he was willing to consider someone forgetting his name *charming*. Still, he sounded fonder than he meant to when he corrected, "It's Bell."

"I knew that. Well, I wrote it in my planner so I wouldn't forget."

Really not charming. Bell felt his lips curl upward without his permission. "Oh really? What happened to the planner?"

"Lost it under a pile of wood shavings, probably. Or else my receptionist put it where it belongs. So… you're sticking around for a while?"

"Depends if I can find a place to live that's not an actual roach motel."

"Uh-huh," Chris said. "Impugning the local attractions already. You'll fit right in. You have the morning free?"

"I guess so," Bell said. "I've already scribbled all over a free map of Pineville, so I know where the highest concentrations of hungover people, high people, and bicycles are located. Figure that's the easiest way to find my future customers."

"Come on over, then. Have you eaten yet?"

"I'm at the diner," Bell said, "where I have eaten enough pancakes to carpet a small studio apartment."

"Tell Owen I said hi."

Bell snorted. "Small town."

"The apartment can be yours for the low, low price of—God, I'll have to text Will and get back to you. He charged the last guy $450 a month, but he had an enormous dog and it scared Lady Frances."

"Who's Lady Frances?" Bell asked as he walked back to the counter and tucked cash under the edge of his plate.

"Shop cat," Chris said. "Hope you're not allergic, but she's skittish and bites pretty much everyone who tries to make her social. So you may never see her."

"Not allergic," Bell said, because he didn't know how to react to the rest of it. "See you in a few." He ended the call, waved to Owen, and went back to his car.

A few minutes later, he pulled into the same spot he'd had the day before. Antonio's was still dark and empty, but it wasn't even ten o'clock. He locked his backpack in the trunk, along with the single suitcase he hadn't bothered to take into the motel, then crossed the street to Good Wood.

The door was unlocked, and the chimes jingled cheerfully when he let himself in. He could hear the whine of a saw blade from the back, so he went around the counter and peeked through the workshop door. Chris was facing the back wall, bent slightly forward as he guided a plank of wood over a table saw. He wore oversize protective earmuffs and safety goggles over his glasses. Bell retreated to the customer side of the counter. It wouldn't do to startle his potential new property manager—and possible friend—in the middle of a task involving extremely sharp blades spinning at high speeds.

To kill time, Bell flipped open the sample binder on the counter. Some of the pieces in the shop were also depicted there, but others were photographed in locations that definitely weren't a dusty, overcrowded showroom. He was so distracted by the fancy houses that held Chris's work that he almost didn't notice the sudden quiet. No more saw blade. "Hey, Chris?"

Chris came through the door, a red stripe still visible on his forehead where the visor had rested. "Sorry about that. I was actually going to go check something in the apartment, but I got sidetracked. You been here long?"

16

Bell shook his head. "Just long enough to see you were working and to be nosy and look at your sample book."

"That's not nosy, it's passive marketing." Chris shrugged. "Word of mouth is the best thing for my line of work. One person gets new furniture or an entertainment unit or a funky lamp, and then their neighbors want them too."

"But bigger and fancier and in nicer wood than everyone else?"

"Exactly." Chris brushed sawdust from his faded T-shirt, which pulled tight across his chest and biceps. "Ugh. You should know that the sawdust gets everywhere in this place. I put a good seal on the apartment door, but there's only so much you can do."

Bell tried not to stare as Chris continued to dust himself off, but it was tough. "I have a hard time believing it's that bad."

"I guess that depends what you're comparing it to. Where'd you sleep last night? Jenny's couch?"

"No, up at the Starlite Cottages."

Chris's eyes widened. "I should have told you about the apartment yesterday, then."

"Jenny suggested it," Bell said. "I mean, you get what you pay for, and it was definitely cheap, even if I didn't go for the 10 percent discount on month-to-month."

"Jenny knows damn well that Scott Taney runs a flophouse. I bet the only reason you didn't end up at her place was that she wanted to see if you'd show up for work today… or didn't want to test whether you'd disappear after stealing her family silver." Chris frowned and reached for the phone. "I don't know what she was thinking."

Bell reached out and put his hand on Chris's wrist. "Don't call. I only took the place a day at a time, and I've got a few leads from the paper." A lie, but he didn't want to seem desperate. "Besides, she doesn't know what I can afford. What if she sent me somewhere and all I had was what she'd paid me and a couple twenties hidden in my suitcase lining?"

Chris sighed as he pulled his hand back from the phone. "I guess. Part of it's that Taney and I have some bad blood from when he didn't pay for some repairs I did and I threatened to call the health board on the motel."

Bell was not going to let himself find Chris's sheepish grin charming, damn it. "What happened?"

"You stayed at the cottages, yeah?" Chris winced. "I should've called the health board anyway, but I was too busy finishing up the renovations upstairs and moving out."

"So where do you live now?"

"I have a little bungalow a few blocks away." Chris ran his hand across his hair, and the sheepish expression reappeared. "I might be sort of a workaholic? When I lived here, I was in the workshop after hours more than I was sleeping, and sooner or later I was going to mess up a project or get myself hurt if I didn't stop that."

Bell raised his eyebrows. "And you don't do anything to your house after work. Nothing at all."

Chris flushed bright red. "Well...."

"Busted," Bell said, crossing his arms and doing his best to frown at Chris.

Chris mirrored his posture and managed to frown about as much as Bell had. "Hey, I'm a property manager now. Always on call. And what are you, the workaholic police?"

Bell snorted, thinking about the guy he was only two weeks earlier—keeping spare suits at the office for when he sweated through the one he wore to work, sleeping at his desk, managing only the occasional Sunday off. "Believe me, I'm not qualified," he said. "So are you gonna show me this place or what?"

Chris shook his head. "I guess I'll show it. Just let me put up my Back in Five sign and I'll take you up."

He led Bell to a set of stairs tucked between the woodshop and the showroom, next to the door for the shop's bathroom. "There's an exterior entrance as well, per code," he said. "But the swallows nest under the roof back there every year, and they make using it a nightmare."

"So you just give tenants a key to your shop?" Bell asked. Was this guy for real? Saving tenants from, what? Tiny angry and/or pooping birds?

"What're they going to do? I take their social security numbers when they move in, and I don't keep cash in the till after hours. It's kind of difficult to steal away with a hundred-pound headboard."

"True," Bell said, trying not to stare at Chris's butt as they ascended. Potential thieves would have to be built like Chris to even attempt it.

"Don't worry, I'll introduce you to Joseph—he minds the shop from time to time, but he's a college kid, so his hours are weird—and Chloe, my co-op student, ditto the weird hours, so they won't think you're breaking and entering. Here we are." Chris turned the key in the lock and opened the door onto a small, bright, clean room.

In his younger days, when the lure of junior consultancy still had him seeing stars, Bell always imagined himself in a spacious, austere high-rise condo, where everything was white walls, metal accents, trendy molded plastic, and black granite—something that would impress his friends and one-night stands. Of course by the time he had saved the money to go look for a place like that, he was working nineteen-hour days and didn't have time for friends or one-night stands. He stayed in the small, tidy, functional two-bedroom he moved into when he became an intern and paid his share of the utilities and cable, even though he rarely used them.

Bell had never envisioned himself in an apartment like this.

The hardwood floors gleamed underfoot, except for the path from the door to the kitchen. At first he thought it was worn, but then he realized it was a trail of sawdust. Maybe Chris had been availing himself of the facilities to make lunch on days he didn't order pizza.

The walls were wood paneled too. Bell had always equated wood paneling with "seventies decorating nightmare." But everything in the apartment seemed to be made of wood, no chrome or plastic in sight: sturdy wood kitchen cupboards, bamboo countertops, mismatched barstools, and a rolltop desk that looked like it might be an antique.

And a bed.

Honestly, Bell hesitated to use the word, because it didn't cover the full effect. The bed, a sturdy four-poster monstrosity that must have weighed several hundred pounds, even before the mountain of pillows and quilts, dominated the room.

For Bell, who was twenty-five and couldn't remember the last time he'd slept with someone, it was basically an invitation to think about sex. Once he laid eyes on it, he could hardly look away.

The bed was designed to be comfortable enough for two people, and two full-grown men, at that. It was also unmistakably sturdy enough to withstand activities more vigorous than sleeping. Bell should've realized that since he'd taken care of his needs for rest, employment, and food, his brain would chime in with a reminder that there were some needs he hadn't taken care of for a long time. He could definitely take care of them here, even if the only company he had was his own hand.

Next to him, Chris cleared his throat.

Bell felt his face heat at being caught daydreaming. He hoped it looked like he'd only been contemplating a good night's rest, but he couldn't make himself meet Chris's eyes to find out.

"So, is there a bathroom?" he said, hoping he sounded more or less normal.

"This way." Chris walked him to the far corner opposite the kitchen area, where a door was slightly ajar. Chris pushed it open a little wider. "After you."

If the main room was cozy warmth and wood, the bathroom was a cool retreat. The walls were wood, but the beadboard was painted glossy white. The floor was made of old-fashioned but immaculately clean small hexagonal tiles, and the fixtures were bright white porcelain, including the enormous claw-foot tub. It had a showerhead mounted to the wall and a curtain that hung from a metal frame attached to the ceiling. It looked complicated enough that Bell was half-afraid he might need instructions. And oh, there his brain went again, thinking about being wrapped in a towel and having to ask for help to get wet.

Bell bit the inside of his cheek, which stung but at least overrode the latest mental detour enough to get his focus away from his overactive, undersupplied libido and back on the apartment.

"'Utilities included' means hot water too?"

"Yeah, as long as you don't go crazy. Water pressure's good. There isn't a washer and dryer, though, so if that's a deal breaker—"

Bell shook his head. "Nope. Already found the laundromat."

"All right," Chris said. "It's yours if you want it. I've got the application downstairs, and it'll be first month's rent plus $300 for the security deposit." He sounded like he might expect Bell to push back, but Bell looked at the tub he wouldn't have to wear flip-flops in, and the casement windows he could open up to let in the breeze. Less than a grand to have a key to a place that didn't smell like must and roach spray was too good a deal to pass up. He held out his hand, and Chris took it in his warm, calloused grip to shake on the deal.

"I've got a checkbook in my pocket," Bell said.

"Well, then, welcome home."

CHAPTER THREE

BELL SAT at the front counter of Good Wood to complete the application while Chris went in the back and, from the sound of it, made some phone calls about pending orders. When Bell finished he slipped the form underneath the ashtray and went out to the car to bring in his stuff from the trunk. It was strange to think everything he had worth keeping fit into a backpack and a medium-size suitcase, but it was kind of comforting too. It really was a new beginning.

Once he'd dropped his bags next to the dresser, Bell pulled out his phone and began a list of everything he needed to do if he was going to stick around Pineville, at least for a little while. He had some time to kill before his shift started. Though the pancakes had made him a bit sleepy and the sunlight filtering through the trees outside filled the room with light and warmth, Bell knew that if he touched the enormous bed, he'd sleep right through work. Especially given the kind of sleep he'd gotten at the Starlite.

Instead he opened his backpack and took out his laptop to set it up in the rolltop desk. Then he took his toiletries kit into the bathroom and unpacked his shampoo and bodywash onto the sill of the frosted window by the tub. He could make do with the microfiber camping towel he'd picked up a few days earlier, but he added towels to his shopping list anyway and went back into the main room to check the kitchenette.

There were plenty of mismatched dishes in the cupboard next to the refrigerator: a mix of colorful melamine plates, square white bowls, and a jumble of actual china in a variety of patterns. The silverware drawer was the same. Bell wondered if it was possible to set his table, even for one, without mixing designs.

His mother would die of embarrassment if she knew, even if Bell was only eating reheated spaghetti for one from a chipped plate with buttercups on it, not serving multiple courses for the ladies at the country club.

The other cupboards were mostly empty, but he found salt, peppercorns, and a remarkable number of spices that were still fragrant.

In contrast to the china cupboard, the shelves under the countertop held high-quality pans and baking dishes, along with a few small appliances. This was more functional than any other kitchen Bell had seen in an apartment—even his coworkers' fancy gourmet kitchens with sleek stainless fixtures—and it made him wish he'd paid more attention when Roberta tried to teach him to cook before he left for college.

Even someone who didn't cook needed the basics, though, so Bell added a few groceries to the shopping list on his phone and went downstairs.

"Hey," he said as he stuck his head into the workshop. "Which grocery store is the good one?"

"Depends," Chris said as he measured a plank and drew marks on it with a carpenter's pencil. "The mercado out past the college has great vegetables, there's a warehouse store and a couple of big-box stores on the highway, and you should probably join the co-op if you want good prices on the bulk bins and fancy olive oil."

"How does a town this small have that many options?" Bell leaned back against a low cabinet.

"College town," Chris said. "Faculty and students are mostly from away, and they expect to find the things they're used to. Plus academic people usually have enough free time to go to a few different stores."

"Where would you recommend for someone who doesn't cook?" Bell smirked. "I'm a whiz at reheating, though."

Chris shook his head. "That sweet little kitchen will go to waste. I'm taking my cast-iron pans home before you ruin them."

"Hey! I can be taught," Bell said. "Or at least our housekeeper tried to teach me, and Antonio showed me some sauce secrets. And I can mostly not ruin eggs."

The corner of Chris's mouth twitched. "Housekeeper? You aren't paying enough rent for housekeeping services, you know."

"I can do my own laundry too," Bell said to sweeten the deal. He grinned and pushed himself up off the cabinet. "I can even iron dress shirts."

"Why on earth would you do that?" Chris looked horrified. "The entire point of living in Pineville is that you never have to iron a shirt again, unless you're a preacher or the president of the college. And I'm pretty sure she wears Birkenstocks to work."

"No Birkenstocks here," Bell laughed. "I should go finish unpacking, though, and run by the motel and drop off the keys before the check-out deadline. Then I can deliver pizzas with a clear conscience, even if I haven't figured out where I'm going to buy my canned spaghetti and sugary cereal."

"I can't believe I rented the apartment to a five-year-old child." Chris shook his head sadly and then turned back to his measurements.

Bell returned upstairs for his wallet and keys, which he'd left in the rolltop desk. When he went to lift the rolltop, though, he realized he wasn't alone.

An enormous striped orange cat was curled up on top of his rolling suitcase, growling softly.

"I thought you were supposed to be shy," Bell accused, creeping forward.

The cat *mrrrow*led. The cadence of its voice and the color of its fur already reminded Bell of Chris, and the white markings around its eyes sort of looked like safety glasses, adding to the likeness.

"Yeah, not so much, I guess." Cautiously he reached out and stroked between the cat's ears.

It jumped to the bed, flopped onto its back, and purred, inviting Bell to stroke the soft fur on its stomach. He wondered if its owner would be so obliging.

Priorities, he reminded himself. Checking out, groceries, work. He gave the cat one last pat on the belly, then shoved his wallet in his pocket and grabbed his keys.

Downstairs, noise from the machinery in the workshop filled the air, as did a gentle drift of sawdust. Bell locked the door to the apartment stairs behind him and turned around only to nearly run into a couple standing at the counter when he went through to the front of the shop. Judging from their neatly pressed clothing, they were from somewhere outside Pineville.

"Excuse me, do you work here?" The woman who asked had green eyes and held herself rigidly, as though a nun might come along at any second and judge her posture.

"Uh, no," Bell said. "Sorry. I just live upstairs."

"We were hoping to speak to someone about a custom dining set," the man, who seemed to be about ten years her senior, put in as if Bell hadn't spoken. "A table and twelve chairs, matching hutch and buffet. Something elegant but understated. Oak, probably, or maybe walnut."

What did this guy expect Bell to do? Smile and say, "Just kidding, I totally work here after all"? Go into the back and grab a complete dining set sample? Bell didn't have experience with custom carpentry, but he wasn't going to stick his nose into the workshop and risk Chris accidentally dismembering himself with a power tool.

He did have experience with marketing, though, and he didn't want to send potential customers away. Besides—yes, there it was. He fished the album out from behind the counter and passed it over. "Why don't you have a look at this and pick out what you like, and you can leave your contact info for a quote?"

Before he could get out the door, though, the noise from the workshop stopped and he gathered the courage to take a look. Chris appeared to be in the process of making a lot of sawdust. Whatever else he was making as a by-product was currently obscured. "Hey," Bell said, sotto voce, stepping back into the workshop. "You've got customers. You want to come sell them an overpriced dining set?"

Chris furrowed his brow. He had a line of sawdust on top of his safety glasses. "Why would it be overpriced?"

"Because they don't seem to care that I don't work here," Bell said dryly.

Chris grinned. "I'll talk them into an upgrade."

That grin made Bell want to stick around, but he had too much to do. "I have to go check out," he said regretfully. "See you tonight, if you're still around."

He hoped he would be.

It took the desk clerk at the motel almost twenty minutes to grumble through a checkout. Apparently he'd been hoping Bell might stay long-term. That didn't leave Bell time to pick up even the basics at any of the grocery stores, so he drove to work and parked around back, next to the Rabbit.

When he opened the kitchen door, Jenny looked up from a vat of pizza sauce. "Well, well. You decided to stick around."

Bell shrugged, feeling awkward about the enthusiasm. "No place better to be," he said, trying for a light tone. He missed.

Jenny tossed him an apron. "If you survived the night at the Starlite, you can survive anything. Scrub up and help me with the sauce. We can't deliver anything until the pizza's made."

Bell made half-a-dozen deliveries before two, which seemed pretty slow. But he'd never delivered pizza before, so what did he know?

Three of his customers asked after Fred. Two of the remaining ones welcomed him to Pineville. The last one, a bent old woman who must have been close to ninety if she was a day, seemed to think he *was* Fred; she patted his cheek and said, "You always were such a nice young man. If I were thirty years younger...."

Bell made a mental note to ask Jenny about her, wished her a pleasant lunch, and booked it back to the pizzeria.

In contrast to those only concerned about Fred, the early dinner eaters were expecting him.

"You must be the new delivery boy," gushed the third suburban mom in a row. "Welcome to the neighborhood. I'm Roxanne."

"Bell." He held out the pizza box. "That'll be $18.50."

It looked like suburban moms were his new bread and butter.

Even better, they gave really nice tips, especially if he flashed a smile or made some friendly comment about the scout troop/soccer team/cheer squad running around the house.

"Playing sports does work up an appetite," one lady said after he'd remarked on the dozen pizzas and the small crowd of children running around on the front lawn. "Do you play any sports, Bill? You look like the athletic type."

Bell wasn't sure if he should correct the name or just back away slowly, but before he could do either, the woman followed up with "Because we could really, really use some assistant coaches at the rec center."

Oh. "I don't know my work schedule yet. But, maybe?" he stammered and resisted the urge to blurt out that he was really sorry he'd thought she was hitting on him. She still thrust a flyer at him as he left, so she must not have thought he was *too* awkward.

In fact, by the end of his shift, Bell had been invited to coach Little League, attend the Trinity Lutheran Men's Supper Club, join the Felix County Bird-Watching Society, and see a Hitchcock film at the college's Retro Movie Night. As he emptied his pockets of change, various flyers, and phone numbers in one of the back booths, Jenny stopped by to chuckle at the pile on the table.

"Looks like you're fitting in already."

"Friendly town." Bell smoothed out the bills and the papers and pushed most of the latter to the side, except for the movie one. That might be interesting, and the *Just $3!* appealed. "Though to be honest, the first time, I thought the woman was hitting on me."

Jenny started to laugh so hard she had to flop down on the seat across from him. "Oh God, Bell. I mean, not that you're a bad-looking guy—"

"Wait a minute," Bell protested, slightly insulted.

Jenny shook her head and wiped at her damp eyes with the back of her hand. "It's not you. It's just that I think you're going to find people here are a bit different than they were in the city. Usually when they ask about you, they really just want to know."

"I'm the pizza guy," Bell said. "How interesting can a pizza guy be?"

"You're the *new* guy," Jenny corrected. "Look. In a town like this, there are two groups of people. There's the college people, and then there's everyone else. The line between them can get kind of blurry. A professor is college people, but her partner might work at city hall, which makes her town people. You're in limbo right now because you're young and working a delivery job, which is kind of college. But you're not living in an overcrowded apartment with a bunch of stoners. Those guys are your customers, not your buddies." She frowned at him. "Where *are* you living? I got a cranky voice mail about you checking out of the Starlite after one night. I know it's a pit, but at least it's cheap."

"About that," Bell said, trying not to blush. "I'm not dead broke. A few years of corporate paychecks and no time to spend them means I'm okay for a while if I budget, but I appreciate you looking out for me."

"Fair enough," Jenny said. "But I'm not going to let you sleep in your car or in the back booth."

"No, I'm good. I was at the diner for breakfast and checked out the classifieds. Made a call and signed a lease this morning."

"Good for you. And good for me too. A lease means you'll be around for a while, at least." She smiled at him. "So, where's home for you now?"

"Across the street?" Bell gave her a sheepish grin as he ran his hand through his hair.

Jenny laughed again. "Oh no, you shouldn't have told me. You're always going to be on call now."

Bell shrugged and repeated his words from earlier. "Not like I have anywhere better to be."

"So you're not going to coach Little League? Take up with the men's choir? Join a stitch-'n'-bitch?" she teased.

"Hey, men can knit," Bell said defensively. Then he shook his head and admitted, "Well, other men, at least."

Grinning, she leaned forward over the table. "Maybe you'll fall in love and spend your days off wooing. Or being wooed."

Bell froze when she mentioned the L word, but he made himself smile. "Anything's possible."

Maybe Jenny sensed that he didn't want to talk about it, because she stood up and ditched her table rag in the laundry bag. "Come on. Let's get out of here. You look like you're running on fumes."

"Believe it or not, I didn't sleep much last night," he said dryly.

"Cockroach steal your covers?"

Bell shuddered. "Don't joke."

Jenny locked up, and Bell trudged across the street. His stomach was rumbling, but he didn't even want to look at another slice of pizza. Maybe there was a convenience store or somewhere else open late where he could get some basic groceries? He'd check it out after he showered off the garlic and oregano.

The water took a minute to heat up, but once it did, Bell forgot all about his stomach and relaxed. The water pressure damn near made him cry. As the layer of pizza grime washed down the drain, so did the tension in his shoulders. He wondered if he could find something to watch on Netflix, or if he should just go to bed to avoid the inevitable return of his hunger.

But he didn't want to go to bed yet. He felt *good*—not drained or wired or grainy-eyed, as he always had when he worked in consulting. Back then, if he made it home, he'd take a five-minute shower and collapse facedown on his bed until his alarm woke him, then peel himself off his sheets and do it all again. Now that he had time and energy for leisure, he wanted to enjoy it.

So he should probably figure out how to get to the nearest convenience store. And in a town the size of Pineville, sooner rather than later. He doubted he'd find much open past midnight.

Bell hurriedly dried himself, scrubbed his towel over his face and hair, and gave the rest of his body a less thorough once-over. He didn't want to put his pizza delivery clothes back on, and his suitcase was still on the bed in the main room.

Oh well, he didn't have a roommate to scandalize—just the cat, and if Lady Frances objected to casual nudity, better to find out now than later. If she was even still around.

Bell was so preoccupied with his plans for his evening of leisure that he didn't notice the guy standing in his kitchen until he'd walked bare-assed over to the bed. Even then it was the sound of something bouncing on the countertop and then rolling onto the floor that made him yelp and turn around.

By sheer dumb luck, he was holding the towel in front of his junk.

"Oh my God," Chris said, flushing crimson. "That'll teach me to call first."

"What are you doing here!" Bell asked, barely managing to keep his voice in the audible-to-humans range.

"I figured you wouldn't have time for groceries because of the customers from this morning." He seemed to be staring determinedly at the bedpost. "I thought I'd get some basics as a housewarming present and a thanks for not telling them to go fuck themselves."

"Oh my God," Bell echoed. Small towns. Seriously. Jenny hadn't been kidding.

"I'm so sorry," Chris continued. "I'll—this wasn't okay, I can't just be using my key to come in whenever—"

"Whenever you buy me groceries?" Now that he was no longer looking for a handy baseball bat to fend off the intruder, the whole situation struck Bell as hilarious. "It's fine. Not like I have anything you haven't seen before, right?"

Chris recovered quickly, but Bell managed to catch his gaze straying to him before he averted it back to the bedpost. His cheeks stayed flushed, though, which made Bell feel oddly flattered.

It probably shouldn't have been flattering, since this was his property manager who had entered his apartment unannounced and interrupted him while he was looking for clean laundry. It probably should have seemed weird. But maybe it had been too long since Bell had noticed any guy looking at him as something other than the junior staffer with the copies or the delivery guy with the pepperoni and extra cheese, because Bell appreciated being appreciated.

He reached for one of the brightly colored quilts folded at the foot of the bed and tried to wrap it around himself in a makeshift toga as subtly as possible given the situation, which probably wasn't at all.

That was confirmed when Chris looked at him and said, "Ohio Star is a good look for you."

"What?"

"The quilt pattern," Chris said, gesturing at Bell. "Ohio Star. Betty McCullough over at the Stop-and-Pick makes them for everyone who asks and some people who don't."

Chris turned back to the kitchen to finish with the groceries as he continued, "So if you're going to be stopping in for a six-pack or a gallon of milk on a regular basis, be prepared to be asked for your color preferences."

Bell felt like he might be in danger of losing the thread of the conversation, but on the other hand, he was pretty much wearing a bedspread and leaving damp footprints on the wooden floor, so he should probably deal with the important parts first. While Chris faced away, he pawed hastily through his suitcase for sweatpants and a T-shirt and slipped back into the bathroom to get dressed. When he emerged Chris was bending over to put something in the fridge. Bell recognized the sound of bottles clanking, and before he could stop himself, he blurted, "Please tell me that's beer."

Chris stepped back from the fridge and held up a brown bottle for Bell's inspection. "Hope you like IPAs."

"I do, actually."

Chris uncapped the bottle, set it on the counter, and pushed it toward Bell, who picked it up to take a long swig. When he set it down, Chris was fussing with something on a cutting board.

"It's a little late for cooking, but I figured you'd be hungry, and this has got to be better than a cup of ramen noodles," Chris said as he turned around. He held up a plate of crackers, slices of cheese, and an apple that had been cut into wedges. "There's a bag of salad and some precut vegetables in the fridge too."

The food reminded him more of an afternoon snack than a real meal, but it looked delicious enough for him to inhale anyway. He had one cheese-topped cracker halfway to his mouth when he remembered his manners. He wasn't sure if he was the host, what with Chris being the manager and grocery buyer, but Bell felt he should offer to share. "You're not having one?" Bell gestured with his beer. "It's really good."

"Local brew. Well, localish." Chris shrugged. "Thanks, but I've got to be getting home. Early day tomorrow. I have a few deliveries to make, but they're small projects, so I don't think I'll be banging around enough to wake you."

Bell nodded and smiled, but he felt a flicker of disappointment. Weird that just a few minutes before, he'd been shocked to find Chris—still almost a total stranger—standing in his kitchen, but now he felt a twinge when Chris said he had to leave. He was going to have to get some sort of social life soon or he'd probably take to hanging around the shop or trying to start meaningful conversations with Lady Frances.

"Well, thanks for the groceries, anyway. I owe you one."

"Hey, I know what it's like to end up living in a small town by accident." Chris wiped down the counter and cleaned the knife he used to make Bell's supper. "Sorry again about letting myself in. I really don't want to be the creepy property guy."

"It's okay," Bell said. "Better than okay, really. I wasn't sure where I was going to get a bite."

"Oh." Chris wiped down the counter once more. "I guess you can only eat pizza so many times in a week."

Bell nodded and then realized Chris was avoiding looking at him again. The back of Chris's neck was flushed pink, and Bell was distracted enough by the sight to miss the first part of what Chris had just said. "Sorry, could you say that again?"

"Nothing important," Chris said. "Just that I should probably get going and that I promise I'll do better about barging into your apartment. I can get my stuff out of here tomorrow, if you want. I shifted a few things up here for storage because part of the shop needed painting."

"Honestly, are you sure you're okay with leaving so much stuff here? Furnished usually just means furniture. This isn't even your place and you're letting me use your kitchen stuff, and your sheets, and—" Bell looked at the quilt, now lying in a rumpled heap in the bathroom doorway. "And apparently I'm repurposing your gift quilt as clothing and then tossing it on the floor. My mother would be appalled."

Chris was laughing when he turned around. "It's fine. Will's a friend of mine, and I'm in the process of renovating at home anyway. Easier without all the extra stuff around. As for the quilt—call it big-city fashion and everyone here would think you're a genius."

Bell couldn't help but notice Chris was still blushing. "That would be a first," he said and then yawned wide enough to make his jaw crack. "Sorry. I swear you're not boring. I just spent last night half-awake being afraid of bugs."

"Did Jenny apologize for sending you to the Starlite?"

"No," Bell said. "You were right, it was a test. Guess I passed, though. She says if I'm living over here, I'm on call all the time."

Chris laughed. "Good thing Antonio's closes at eleven, then." He picked up a reusable shopping bag Bell hadn't noticed earlier. "I'll head out. Let me know if there's anything you need? I have boxes and boxes of random things at the house, so before you go buying stuff, just ask."

Most of the stuff Bell really needed, money couldn't buy. Or, well, it could, but it was illegal in a lot of states. "I'll keep that in mind," he promised. "Thanks again."

He tried not to stare at Chris's ass as he left. Really.

He finished off his snack and IPA while he looked for something good on Netflix. A little aimless browsing led him to the pilot episode of *Schitt's Creek*, but when he gleefully imagined his mother as the leading lady and thought about starting the next episode, he decided he might as well finish unpacking. His casual clothes fit neatly into the heavy, chunky tallboy against the wall. The few dress shirts and other textile trappings he'd held on to from his previous life would need to hang up, though. Hopefully the closet would offer some space—he'd forgotten to check when he first viewed the apartment.

The closet door creaked when he opened it, and Bell made a note to pick up a can of WD-40 or something. But there was a long metal bar across the space, with plenty of room for the two suits he'd kept and a few pairs of trousers and collared shirts. Bell hung everything up—he'd worry about wrinkles and dry-cleaning if he ever had occasion to need business casual here—and was lining up his dress shoes on the floor when he noticed the box.

Frowning, Bell pushed his shoes to one side and tugged the blue Rubbermaid container toward the opening of the closet. This must be the thing Chris planned to move, or maybe the previous tenant had left it. Curiosity got the better of him, and Bell brushed off a thin layer of sawdust and pried open the lid to find a container full of—

Bell resisted the impulse to reach inside to touch. It was probably poor etiquette to put your mitts all over someone else's collection of artisanal wood dildos. And he was pretty sure that's what he'd found. The Rubbermaid tub held a dozen or so phallic objects ranging in size from "cute" to "yes, please" to "definitely not," in various styles and types of wood, some curved, some straight, some twisted or ridged, all polished to a high gloss.

Bell thought it unlikely Chris had left these for him. If he had, that was absolutely weird, and Bell needed to find a new place to live. Potentially on the other side of the country.

He put the lid back on the box and decided he should go to bed.

But when he had relieved himself, brushed his teeth, washed his face, and climbed into bed, he couldn't sleep. The sheets smelled fresh, and the mattress made him feel like he was being cradled by the Stay Puft Marshmallow Man. He didn't have to listen to a drippy bathroom faucet all night like at the Starlite, and he *should* have been tired. He'd worked a full day and then spent time unpacking.

His brain wouldn't shut off. He kept making lists—things he had to do the next day, ways he might keep busy over the weekend, official documents he'd need to change his address on. Every time he got more than three items down the list, a flashing neon sign popped up in his brain, proclaiming *Chris McGregor's Handmade Artisanal Dildo Collection!!*

The third time it happened, Bell rolled over and groaned into a soft, fluffy pillow.

The bed didn't make a sound. The mattress didn't shift. The frame didn't creak.

Bell lifted his head and ran a hand over the wood post. Someone had spent a lot of time on this bed to make sure the pieces fit perfectly and that it would stand up to rigorous use.

Okay, fine. Chris had spent a lot of time on it. Sweet, sexy Chris—Bell had never been into beards, but he could make an exception—had built this enormous bed with his own two apparently

34

very capable hands, and he obviously had sex in mind. And not slow, tender, quiet sex either. Loud, hard, frantic, can't-get-enough sex. Bruised-the-next-day sex. Clawing-at-the-sheets sex.

Bell rolled onto his back again before he could lose the rest of his dignity and start to hump the mattress. He'd been out of the game for too long if a bed could induce that level of sexual tension.

Well. A bed and a box full of dicks.

Fuck it. At least jerking off would help him fall asleep.

CHAPTER FOUR

THE MORNING sun shone stubbornly through the window, and Lady Frances very nearly matched its ferocity as she patted Bell's nose with the very tips of her claws exposed.

Startled by both sun and cat, Bell sat up abruptly, causing Lady Frances to jump down and meow with irritation. "Oh, hey," he said. "How did you get in here? Pretty sure I closed the door last night. Also pretty sure I don't have any cat food."

Lady Frances jumped back up on the bed and swatted Bell's leg. Then she leaped off and headed for the kitchenette, where she sat down in front of a lower cupboard, tucked her tail neatly around her feet, and glared at him.

"Okay, okay," Bell said and managed to untangle his legs from the quilt without falling off the bed. He was a little wary of being naked around the cat, especially because she looked like she might attack his junk if he didn't find some cat food soon. Bell leaned down to open the cupboard, which turned out to be the home of a plastic container and a white ceramic dish with a colorful fish painted on the bottom.

Lady Frances twined around Bell's ankles while he put a handful of food into her dish, and then he found a teacup to fill with water. Once she was settled and eating, he went to get dressed and figure out what to do on his day off.

Unfortunately his shoes were in the closet, sitting next to the Rubbermaid container. Bell had intended just to grab them and run, but he couldn't help but open the lid again and look at the dildos. They were pretty, which was a weird thing to think about sex toys, but Bell had never seen anything like them. He strayed back to his thoughts from the night before, but he managed to get the lid snapped onto the container before he ended up back in bed, trying out the merchandise—maybe the slim one just a bit wider than his thumb, or the one with the slight bumps that looked like it would skim his prostate and make him beg for more.

That was not a productive line of thought. Not if he wanted to buy his own groceries and get some laundry done—and buy some lube. He stepped into his sneakers and went downstairs.

Chris was in the shop with a teenage girl with pink hair and sneakers, packing boxes with wooden bowls of all sizes—from tiny ones that might hold a few trinkets to large salad bowls that could serve a family. "Morning," Chris said and smiled at Bell.

The girl looked up too. "This the new guy?"

Bell hadn't expected to see Chris, even though he had fair warning that Chris might be in the shop this early. The warring images of fantasy Chris and morning-reality Chris were making him a little dizzy. But he needed to get a grip if he had to meet new people, and a kid, at that. "You can call me Bell."

She smiled back. "Chloe. I'm the peon."

Chris rolled his eyes at her. "You're a brat who is not allowed to operate power tools without supervision, because I like having an insurable business. Stop whining about the sweeping and staining." While Chloe was still grinning unrepentantly, Chris turned to Bell. "There's coffee if you want it?"

"Um, sure." Chris wore a soft, well-loved flannel shirt over a blue T-shirt that made his eyes sparkle. Maybe if Bell got some coffee, he could stop staring at him. He poured his cup slowly and got himself under control.

"Did you sleep well?"

"Yeah," Bell said. "Had a little trouble getting to sleep, and then Lady Frances woke me up by punching me in the nose—"

Chloe made an offended noise. "Oh, she did not." She stacked the boxes and walked toward the garage door at the back.

Chris, however, looked perfectly credulous.

"—but other than that it was golden. That bed's a miracle."

"Sorry about Lady Frances," Chris said. "I honestly thought she'd be shy, at least at first, though I should have known she's used to getting her own way. Did you find the food?"

"She showed me," Bell said and sipped his coffee. "This is really good, by the way."

"Friend of mine roasts it. He's got a little shop up by the college, but it's always busy, so I just buy beans from him and make it here. Anything you need me to bring in for you, or anything that's in the way?"

"Um," Bell said again and set his coffee down carefully, in case he spilled it all over somebody's expensive buffet. He cast a look toward Chloe's retreating back. "There's a bin in the closet—"

"Oh fuck," Chris said quietly as he followed Bell's gaze. He set down his own coffee and flushed bright red. "I am so sorry. I was absolutely certain I'd taken that to the house—I put it there because, well." He nodded toward Chloe. "I have no idea what you must think of me at this point, breaking into your apartment with cheese and my shop cat assaulting you, and…. Wait. Did you actually open it?"

"Yes?" Bell ruffled his hair and made himself look at Chris, though he hoped his voice didn't squeak. "Dude, how are you not a zillionaire from your Etsy shop?"

"What Etsy shop?"

Chloe opened the garage door and piled the boxes into the bed of a pickup parked there. "The one where you sell your artisanal, organic, hand-waxed wooden dildos," Bell said slowly. "Because you have one, right? An Etsy shop, I mean. You have more than one wooden dildo. Not that I looked—well, okay, I did look, but the point here is that you should be selling them."

"No," Chris said. "I sell bowls and tables, and sometimes headboards with spindles that break on the lathe, and I like to whittle, and there is no way you are getting me to open an online shop."

"Of course not," Bell said. "You'd suck at it. You still use a restaurant order pad to give people handwritten receipts with carbon copies for your records!" He'd seen the pad next to the perfectly good front desk computer, which he could only assume was so Joseph-who-minded-the-shop-sometimes could play solitaire. "That would be my job."

Chris took a deep breath. "You already have a job."

"I have flexible hours." Bell frowned at Chris. "You have a talent. Use it."

"Oh God," Chris said. "How do you know I have a talent? You didn't—"

Oh my God. Bell's face had to be crimson. "No! I didn't— you don't just go around doing quality checks on other people's sex toys!" Even if you thought about it. Even if you *fantasized* about it. "Especially not if you, like, have concerns about splinters and, uh, other sanitary issues."

Chris frowned and led Bell away from Chloe and into the storefront, where he—oh Lord—pulled yet another artful sex toy from a bin under the counter and handed it over. "Does this look like it's going to give you splinters?" He sounded offended.

Bell didn't *want* to look at his super-hot super's handmade dildo. Not with his super-hot super right there, probably reading the litany of profane thoughts marching through Bell's brain via the expression on his face. But his hand reached out without his permission, and soon he found himself not just *looking* at the thing but also *holding* it.

It was surprisingly heavy and very smooth, curved in a gentle S shape and tapered at one end in an obvious handle. It gleamed. The reflection of light off the varnish was almost mesmerizing.

"Uh," he said as he frantically tried to remember the question and not his fantasy from the night before. It didn't help to speculate about why Chris had a dildo under the counter in his shop. "Uh, I'm sorry I impugned the integrity of your sanding process," he finally managed.

Now give it back, he coached his hand. *Or just—put it down on the counter or—*

Chris took it from him. "Don't forget the finish. There's ten coats on that thing."

"Ten coats of *what*? I mean, I'm pretty sure most of what you coat furniture with is strictly for external use."

Lord, why couldn't he shut his stupid mouth? He wanted to put an end to the sex toy conversation, not prolong it. Maybe Chloe would come find them and put him out of his misery.

"Medical-grade polymer coating. It's in my supplier's catalog." Chris shrugged. "People use it for wooden body piercings and, uh, other things."

"Oh."

Chris put the dildo back under the countertop, and Bell relaxed. "Not just wax, huh?"

"That would definitely not be sanitary. Not waterproof, and probably also not good for internal use."

Before he could think better of it, Bell said, "Wait, so you *do* use them?"

Chris looked caught, frozen in Bell's sights with his eyes wide and his mouth slightly open.

Bell covered his face with his palms. His imagination didn't need that knowledge. "Never mind. Let's pretend I didn't ask that. Actually let's pretend this conversation never happened and go back to the part where you asked if anything was in my way."

When he peeked through his fingers, he saw Chris smiling ruefully, his ears still pink. "Anything you need, or anything I left in your way?" he repeated dutifully.

"Yes," Bell said and removed his hands from his face. "There's a bin of sex toys of uncertain provenance in the closet. Are you hoarding them for a reason, or can I set up an online shop and sell them on Etsy? My cut is 35 percent."

Chris shook his head. "Go for it, I guess, if it means that much to you."

Jesus, didn't he know he was supposed to negotiate? "Awesome. Now I have a project for the weekend." Bell finished the rest of his coffee just as the clock ticked over to 9:00 a.m. and Chris went to the front door. "One piece of advice, though?"

Chris looked back over his shoulder as he unlocked the door. "What?"

"Keeping a dildo under the counter is weird, dude. Like, you got rid of the ones in the back because of Chloe, but you decided to keep that one around?"

Chris flushed. "I just finished this one yesterday. I was going to bring it home once the last coat of varnish dried."

Well, that didn't help at all. Now Bell would spend all day thinking about what he planned to do with it.

BELL DIDN'T start on the Etsy page that weekend. He was too busy changing his address, unpacking, and getting the lay of the land, so to speak. On Saturday evening he and Jenny went to Retro Movie Night and sat in the back, but they ended up talking the whole time about Jenny's awful ex-boyfriend, until the usher kicked them out. They went back to his apartment instead, and Lady Frances eyed Jenny distrustfully from across the room with her tail twitching, while Jenny laughed at Bell's impression of his mother.

"Is she really that bad?" Jenny asked, wiping up the condensation ring from one of the IPAs Chris had bought.

Bell let out a long breath and thought about it. "I don't know. It might just be that it was too much to handle her on top of everything else, I guess. Ask me again when I have more emotional distance."

"And when will that be?"

"When I stop waking up at five in the morning panicking that I've slept in, maybe." *When I've decided I can actually tell her the truth about my job.* Maybe more ifs than whens, now that he thought about it.

Sunday, miraculously, he slept in and made the executive decision to do nothing. He watched six episodes of *Schitt's Creek*, logged in and out of his bank account a few times just to assure himself that he didn't have to go back to his old life if he didn't want to, and ordered takeout from a sandwich shop.

By the time his next day off rolled around, Bell's towel situation had gotten dire, and the few groceries he'd picked up before work on Monday had dwindled. Friday morning he hit the road in the Malibu and checked out the co-op and one of the big box stores.

When Bell got back to Good Wood with his groceries, Chris was deep in conversation with two women. Bell resisted the urge to eavesdrop when he heard "kids' bunk bed" followed by "pirate ship," but as he climbed the stairs to his apartment, he reminded himself to ask Chris about it later and maybe see if Chris could show him any sketches. For a few months when Bell was a kid and his parents were waiting to close on a house, he had shared a room in their temporary apartment with Cam, and while it was a nice room with matching twin beds and bookcases, their parents never would have gone for anything fanciful, like beds that looked like boats or animals or trees.

Lady Frances supervised Bell as he put his groceries away, but didn't answer when Bell asked her what other furniture Chris had made.

Bell didn't ask the cat about the dildos. He did think about them, though, as he had off and on for the past week—both in a professional and a more abstract sense. He made himself a turkey sandwich and munched on some carrot sticks while his laptop booted up. Lady Frances slunk off when she realized nothing more was coming from the kitchen.

Bell dragged out the container of wooden toys—he'd told Chris that he might as well leave them there if Bell was going to design a marketing scheme for them—and then pulled up several tabs in his browser.

The first was an Etsy-for-beginning-sellers blog that had a lot of tips about practical things. Bell bookmarked it and then moved on to some actual shops that sold handcrafted sex toys and bondage gear. He was pleased to see that a number of them were really tastefully done, with nice photographs and descriptions of the materials and the processes. They were interesting—almost soothing—reading. He bookmarked a shop that did floggers and whips, because the site was well done and the products, with their braided handles and colorful leather, were really pretty.

The next page showed actual dildos. The shop's avatar photo was just a close-up of something in silicone, ridged and purple. So when Bell clicked through, he wasn't expecting what he found. Bell blinked and then clicked to enlarge the image. He squinted. It looked like some sort of alien squid, with bulbous green eyes and—he blinked again—tentacles, complete with suckers, coiled around the base of the toy. It was weird. And big. Weird and big and purple. With eyes. Bell couldn't help but wonder if that could possibly feel not-weird, much less good, going into him, especially when it was covered in lube, which would only make it look *more* alien. Was that part of the appeal? He squirmed uncomfortably but couldn't manage to stop the train of thought.

His phone trilled with an incoming call, jerking Bell from his thoughts about getting fucked by the alien dildo. He looked down at his notification screen.

Mom calling.

Oh Jesus. *There* was a juxtaposition he never needed. He steeled himself for the potential worst and accepted the call. "Hi, Mom."

"Hi, sweetheart," his mother said warmly.

Bell tried to relax. It would probably help if he could stop staring at the sea monster dildo, so he closed that window. But that left him looking at the paddles, and—no.

He closed the laptop.

"I'm just calling to check in. How are you, baby?"

Bell winced. His mother never "just" called. She made itineraries for small talk. "I'm doing well." He would've said *I'm good* if he were talking to anyone but family. "I found a new job and a place to live. I'm not, like, living on the street or whatever you're panicking about."

"Bellamy Alexander," his mother said disapprovingly. That didn't take long. "I'm your mother. Of course I worry about you. That's what mothers do."

He wouldn't have cared if she ever stopped at worry.

"Sorry, Mom," he said automatically. He didn't have the energy to fight with her.

"And what's this about a new job?"

Bell winced and wondered how best to spin it. "I found something with a couple local small-business entrepreneurs. It's not what I'm used to. More a little bit of everything—logistics, advertising, networking."

"That doesn't sound like very stable work," his mother said doubtfully. "Are you sure you're happy there? Margaret Dawson's firm is looking for someone to join their junior management team—"

Bell rubbed the bridge of his nose and tried to stave off a headache. "I'm sure, Mom. I have a lease on an apartment and everything. I made a commitment. Okay?"

His mother made a noise that indicated they would revisit the matter later, when she'd had time to prepare a more elaborate verbal assault. "Have you spoken to your brother and sister lately? I know they've been thinking about you."

When? Bell wondered. They both worked fifteen-hour days. "No," he said. "I've been working. Unpacking. Doing a little market research. How are they doing?"

"Well, you know Emily's been putting in those long hours for that pharmaceutical account? All that work finally paid off and they're putting her in charge of it, effective immediately, with a retroactive pay raise."

"That's great," Bell said, mustering up what he hoped was sufficient false enthusiasm. His sister might actually be happy about spending more of her life indoors, staring at a computer screen. Who knew anymore?

"But that isn't the best news." His mother lowered her voice conspiratorially. "I probably shouldn't tell you this"—Bell wished that would stop her—"but Monica is pregnant." She paused. "You're going to be an uncle again!"

"Wow. Another grandkid, huh? Congratulations, Mom," Bell said. He meant it, mostly. Cam might have chosen the kind of life Bell left behind, with too many working hours and not enough downtime, but he loved his wife. They were good parents, probably, or would be, if Cam stopped working so much overtime.

That didn't make the news much easier to hear, though. In the face of his siblings' accomplishments this week, Bell finding a pizza-delivery job and an apartment he could afford seemed paltry. Even if *he* was satisfied with them, his parents never would be.

"Oh Lord, baby. Don't use the G-word," his mother said. "They can call me Mimi or something when they're old enough to talk."

He took a deep breath and lied through his teeth. "I have to go, Mom, I'm getting a work call. I'll talk to you later, okay?"

He got off the phone, looked around at his empty apartment and his half-eaten sandwich, and sighed.

Fuck it. So what if he was already fulfilling his own prophecy about spending too much time in the workshop? He tucked his laptop under his arm and went downstairs to find some company.

Chris was sitting at the counter with a pile of paper scraps and a calculator that looked old enough to have been bought for his sixth-grade math class. Bell could smell the burned scent of what was left in the coffeepot, so he emptied it and started a fresh one. Chris was too busy sorting the scraps into different piles and muttering to himself to notice when Bell took his cold mug upstairs to wash.

While he was up in his kitchen, he grabbed his sandwich and—what the hell, why not? He owed Chris after the snack the other night—made another one for Chris.

By the time he got back to the showroom, the coffee was ready and Chris's mutters had turned to a quiet, steady stream of insults at a wide variety of what sounded like both vendors and customers. When Bell slid the turkey sandwich and a fresh cup of coffee onto the counter, Chris startled and stared at him. "What are you doing here?"

"Bringing you lunch? You made me dinner the other night. Plus, your coffee was ancient, so I ran a new pot." Bell held up his own plate. "My mom called before I got very far into my own lunch."

Chris shoved the papers aside, ignoring that half of them fluttered to the floor. "Come on, sit down and keep me company. Chloe's got a basketball game, and Joseph's got a paper due. How's your mom?"

"Checking in to see where I stand in the Alexander children rankings." Bell shrugged and took a bite of his sandwich. "My brother's having another baby—okay, his wife, but still—and my sister just got a raise that was apparently retroactive to the Clinton administration."

"Ouch," Chris said. "How does she feel about your journey of self-discovery?"

"Like I should get back home and either go to law school or get back into consulting, but this time at a boutique firm her tennis partner owns." Bell shook his head. "I don't think she'll ever understand why I gave notice. 'Alexanders don't have personal crises, darling.'"

Chris wrapped his hands around his mug. "But are you actually having a crisis, or are you just doing your own thing?"

"No idea," Bell said, thinking of the weeks of late nights putting together proposals for projects and clients he didn't care about. Feeling like no one else had really cared about them either. *Was* he having a crisis, or just freeing himself from mind-numbing tedium? "I just told her I was consulting for small local specialty businesses and that I'd signed a lease."

"Both of which are true," Chris said. "And if you don't have too many plans for the afternoon, I'll hire you to help me get my billing in order before scraps of paper take over the entire living space and you and Lady Frances have to move into my basement." He tipped his head to one side, thinking. "Or attic. Which one is less creepy?"

"Attic," Bell said. "At least with the attic, I have the cachet of some exotically deranged literary figure."

"Not to mention the attic is less murderous," Chris mused. "And less sex dungeony."

"You'd think some enterprising architect would try to make their name by designing something with more light. Like a sex sunroom or something."

Chris grinned. "Well, sadly I have neither. Just a plain old attic and a plain old basement. They both have spiders. So, what do you say? Give me a hand with this paperwork? I'll pay you."

Bell pretended to give it serious thought. "I don't know," he said slowly. "I'm already billing hours in the local food-and-beverage sector. Can you make it worth my while?"

"I'll pay you what you're worth," Chris promised, and his lips quirked. "Plus dinner as a thank-you?" His flirty smile turned into a wry grimace. "I may have been putting this off for a while. It could be time-consuming."

"I like a challenge." One of the few things Bell could stand about his last job was getting to solve an actual problem. "Give me your worst and tell me where you want me to set up. And you"—

Bell pointed at him—"are responsible for supplying the coffee from here on out."

Chris smiled. "I think I can handle that. Maybe we can start in the office and move somewhere more comfortable when the shop closes?" Then he made another face. "God. That was almost as bad as the basement/attic comment."

"It's an offer too good to refuse, so I'll just have to live with the risk that you'll drag me off for some nefarious purpose. Besides, I can handle myself." Bell didn't wink, but he thought about it.

Chris rolled his eyes. "I promise I'll have you in bed by curfew." He motioned to Bell's laptop. "Need anything before we get started? Or do you just want to bring this back to the office?"

Bell flushed a bit at the insinuation. He had thought that Chris's innuendos were inadvertent slips of the tongue, but now he wondered if Chris had been throwing those lines to him on purpose. If so, Bell was definitely up for a game of catch.

"I won't know until I see what I'm working with." Bell gestured in front of him and picked up his computer. "So you might as well lead the way."

Chris led him into a room that Bell supposed could, technically, be called an office. A desk filled up a large portion of the space and was accompanied by a chair in front and one behind. Plastic stackable drawer-things labeled with the alphabet took up one corner. The desk held another computer, even newer-looking than the one up front. It presumably came with a keyboard and mouse and other accoutrements, though it was difficult to tell with all the tools, wood shavings, cans of stain, paintbrushes, and other woodworking detritus around it.

Bell didn't need feng shui to identify the problem here.

Chris stepped around to the slightly battered leather chair behind the desk, picked up an old ledger, brushed a feathered cat toy off it, and then made a show of dusting the cover off with his hand. "This is where the magic happens."

"I hate to tell you this, but I'm pretty sure all this crap didn't get here by magic." Bell waved his hand to encompass the mess.

47

"Fair," Chris agreed, taking a battered cardboard box from the floor. He swept most of the top of the desk into it. "As opposed to how I'm treating Will."

"What do you mean?" Bell frowned at the self-reproach in Chris's tone.

"We set up my rent for the shop based on my profits, and neither one of us is super great at keeping up with the accounting. Funny, given he has a PhD in math, but that's where we are. We've been kind of guesstimating the rent." Chris finished with the sigh of the overwhelmed.

"I can see we're working with an unorthodox office-management approach," Bell said in his best consultant tone. "But we here at the Alexander Group will find a solution to meet your needs and those of your stakeholders."

"The Alexander *Group*?" Chris asked, gesturing at Bell standing alone.

"My colleague Lady Frances will be assisting." Bell picked up the feather toy. "It's a cross-disciplinary approach."

Chris chuckled and muttered something about discipline that Bell didn't catch.

Bell cleared his throat, slid into the seat across from Chris, and opened the laptop so they could both see as Chris plopped a stack of paperwork down next to it. "So," Chris began, and then his face went a bit pink as the laptop screen flashed on. "Speaking of discipline."

Oh God. "That was market research," Bell protested, but he could feel the heat of his own blush as he closed out several windows of sexual paraphernalia Etsy shops. He could find them again later using the history feature.

"You're certainly multitalented."

Bell shrugged. "I'm decent at the business stuff, but there's a lot I don't know anything about." He pointed at a carved wooden box that was obviously Chris's handiwork. "I'm not really good with my hands."

"Maybe I can give you a crash course sometime," Chris said, his expression wry to the point of absolute self-awareness.

At this rate Bell was going to die of sexual tension before dinner. "I might have to take you up on that. But first, business. What exactly are we doing?"

"I'm not past due on any bills or anything like that. I'm okay with keeping up with what I owe, and I generally keep up with what I've spent for Will on maintenance and renovations."

Generally keep up with seemed like a recipe for disaster or, at the very least, like a serious disagreement waiting to happen. "Sounds like you lucked out on the landlord," Bell prompted.

Chris scrubbed his fingers through his hair. "Not luck, really. Will and I have been friends since the fates of college housing put us in the same suite freshman year, where we forged an early bond over a mutual love for soccer and the local diner as well as a mutual loathing for the other guys in our suite."

Bell waved his hand in a go-ahead motion. It wasn't totally necessary from a business perspective, but anything that shed more light on what made Chris tick was something Bell wanted to know.

"The other guys not being the type that appreciated the fine qualities that the math nerd and the gay nerd gave to their living space. Especially after the motley crew of Flotsam and Jetsam— that was literally our team name—crushed theirs in the intramural soccer cup."

Bell had to chuckle at the mental image his brain conjured of Chris and Will, somehow in plaid and tweed respectively, hollering and raising a trophy over their heads together. "Okay, so Will isn't likely to be a problem, though we obviously still need to get on top of that. What about the other stuff?"

"I probably have some folks that owe me for some installments, but the thing is, I don't know for sure. You'd think I'd—" He shook his head. "Never mind."

"So matching payments and invoices," Bell said. "Awesome. You have a spreadsheet for this somewhere? QuickBooks or something? Or are we starting from scratch?"

Chris handed him the ledger and a few folders with dog-eared invoices sticking out. "Does this count as from scratch?"

Oh boy. "Maybe you should bring the coffee pot in here," Bell suggested with a hint of trepidation, only partly kidding, and then started to sort through the receipts.

"How bad is it?" Chris asked a few minutes later, when he returned with the coffee.

Bell didn't look up. "I've seen worse."

"Really?"

"No," Bell admitted, and Chris choked as he tried to swallow a sip of coffee.

"I have other talents?" He made it a question.

"Definitely. And don't think I'm going to let you near the books for What Wood You Do."

"What I would—"

"The Etsy shop."

"Shouldn't that be What Wood Do You?" Chris asked as Bell finished the first sort—alphabetical.

"We can talk once we've worked through this mess." Bell picked up the *A*s and waved them at him.

Chris sighed and dropped into his desk chair. "You can tell me the truth. I'm already embarrassed."

Bell shrugged. "You're a sole proprietor with limited employees. If this were a bigger operation, it would be a bigger deal." He wrapped his hands around his mug and frowned at Chris. "But dude, what about the money? Do you take a salary?"

It was Chris's turn to shrug. "More like a commission, I guess? I don't write myself a regular check."

"Okay. So your regular bills are pretty much the insurance and utilities. Everything else is ad hoc—materials, tools, your cut. And your receivables, I can whip into shape."

"Is that what you needed that website for?" Chris teased weakly. "That sounds like a pain in the ass."

"Ha-ha," Bell said. "Whatever you're planning for dinner better be good, because I'm going to be hungry."

"Do you want me to stay here or get out of your hair?" Chris reached for the ledger, but Bell shook his head and smiled.

"Let me do a first blind pass to see what's going on. Go sand a table or something."

CHAPTER FIVE

WHEN CHRIS escaped to the workshop, Bell pulled the papers closer and got to work. It wasn't all that terrible once he got into it. There was a lot of paper, but that was better than having stuff missing. It wasn't too difficult to organize things and set up a system so *keeping* them organized wouldn't be a challenge in the future.

He decided to count himself lucky Chris hadn't signed up for paperless billing. Though maybe they could look into that in the future, when Bell had drilled some organizational principles into his head. In the meantime Chris was not allowed anywhere near the books for WWYD. He could participate in setup by doing sexy write-ups about the kinds of wood he used. He certainly had skill with innuendo.

Bell stacked the invoices and the ledger and put them under a rough chunk of wood that was apparently a paperweight, or possibly a future item to be sold online, then went into the shop. "Phase one complete," he said. "Tomorrow I'll put this into a spreadsheet and start creating overdue invoices, but that's enough for now."

"That was, um… way faster than I expected," Chris said, pushing away from a table that apparently actually needed sanding. "I seriously can't thank you enough, but if you're hungry, I can at least get started on that dinner I promised." He looked at his watch. "It's after five anyway. Time for me to go. Joseph can handle any customers who come window shopping."

Bell's stomach growled. "Uh. I guess I'm hungrier than I thought. Dinner sounds great." What would be better, though, was if he could tell whether Chris meant it as a "thanks for the favor" dinner or an "are you interested in getting in my pants" dinner. But only time and/or uncomfortable directness would answer that question for sure. "Should I change, or…?"

"If you want. It's not like I've got a dress code or anything. But no shoes in the house, because I just refinished the floors."

Bell followed Chris out the back to a Ford pickup, old but obviously well cared for. That was something—besides the obvious ledger book—Bell had noticed about Chris. Everything he truly cared for was very well maintained. The pillows and quilts in Bell's room were clearly vintage, but nothing was wrinkled or stained, and Chris's work tools were gleaming and rust-free. Then there were his actual pieces. They were carefully carved, assembled, and sanded.

The truck started on the first try and thrummed happily to life as soon as Chris turned the key... and wow, Bell needed to stop being jealous of inanimate objects. That was a little absurd. "Nice truck," he commented. An old-fashioned red-and-yellow-checked blanket covered the worn leather seats, and Bell couldn't help but run his hand over it as he buckled up. The blanket didn't say "Chris" to him.

"Heirloom, I guess you could say," Chris answered his unspoken question. "It and the truck belonged to my grandfather." He smiled a little. "He believed in regular maintenance and fixing things that weren't all the way broken."

"Sounds like you take after him."

Chris gave him a sideways glance as they pulled onto the road. "I guess so. I never did see the point of buying something completely new when you've already got something that's just as good, maybe even better, with a little work."

It was too tempting to pursue that line of conversation to find out if that was how Chris felt about relationships too. "So, you live far?"

Chris colored. "Uh... not really." He took a left turn down a quiet residential street. Then again all the streets were quiet compared to what Bell was used to. "It's close enough to walk, but if I have to walk past the diner, I always end up stopping. Especially if it's pancake day."

Bell laughed. "That's fair."

"The house actually belonged to my grandfather too. But uh, it's not in the same shape as the truck." He glanced over out of the corner of his eye. "I apologize in advance."

Chris seemed to turn wistful at that admission, so Bell didn't ask anything else. He had prepared himself for something ramshackle, but Chris pulled into a driveway attached to a brick bungalow that admittedly needed some TLC. It was still charming, even if Bell could see signs of age as well as repairs that obviously weren't Chris's handiwork. The roof looked newish, but the trim on the windows needed painting, and judging from the pile of rubble and the wooden stairs by the front door, the old porch was in the process of being replaced. Bell eyed the makeshift stairs dubiously. Definitely not Chris's craftsmanship.

Chris caught him looking and huffed a smile. "Don't worry, we're going in the side door."

Bell followed Chris around to the left and got a peek at the detached garage and an overgrown garden in the back. The side door led into a kitchen that had been refurbished, if not by Chris himself, then probably at his direction. Butcher-block countertops and perfect, straight, gleaming dark wood cabinets and stainless appliances made up for what might otherwise have been a conspicuous lack of space. A cloth cubby of guest slippers hung on the wall.

"Make yourself at home," Chris directed and nodded at a shoe rack by the door.

Bell toed off his shoes and helped himself to the bright pink slippers in hopes of garnering a smile. "So what's for dinner?" he asked, debating between hopping up on the counter and sitting at the kitchen table like a civilized adult. He opted for the chair. Maybe he could work up to the counter.

Chris opened the fridge and rummaged. "Umm, let's see. Stir fry? Quesadillas? Potpie?"

"Potpie," Bell said firmly as his stomach growled. God. The last time he'd had home-cooked comfort food....

Chris looked down at Bell's middle and grinned. "So now that I know what it takes to keep the bookkeeping going," he said as he turned back to the counter, "if I offer you a beer or tell you I might have some leftover brownies, what will that get me?"

Bell bit his lip to avoid saying that Chris could have whatever he wanted from Bell if he wanted it enough to ask for it. "I'll take dictation of descriptions of your kinky sex-toy art," he offered instead. He'd left the laptop in the truck, though. "But no business until after food. Do you need help with anything?"

Chris pulled a few containers from the fridge. "Nah. Most of this is putting together leftovers. It might be a while for potpie, though. You want to start with a brownie?"

"Beer and a brownie," Bell said after some thought. "If I'm gonna stuff myself full of carbs with potpie, I might as well go all the way."

Chris pulled a plate of thick, fudgy brownies out of an old-fashioned tin breadbox, then opened two beers and handed one to Bell. "Porter goes nicely with chocolate."

God, that brownie looked amazing and smelled even better—rich and cocoa-y. Bell touched his beer bottle to Chris's, took a sip, and contemplated the plate of chocolatey temptation. He needed to put something *in* his mouth before something embarrassing came *out* of it.

"Cut one of those in half first, okay? Too much sugar and I'll fall asleep before you finish making supper." Bell's stomach rumbled again.

"Fair enough," Chris said, handing half a brownie to Bell. "I'll use up all the chicken, then. A growing boy needs his protein."

Bell paused with the brownie just touching his lips. He was furiously glad he hadn't yet put it in his mouth, because he'd definitely be choking. "I do get cranky when I don't eat right."

"Can't have that," Chris said and smiled.

Bell took a bite. Dark chocolate with a hint of coffee exploded on his tongue. He reminded himself it was too soon to propose marriage, no matter how good the brownie. "Is there anything you *don't* make from scratch? Because these have never seen the inside of a box," Bell said, trying to stop himself from cramming the rest into his mouth and licking his fingers.

55

"Not much," Chris said. The back of his neck flushed red, and Bell found it hard not to stare. "I mean, I bake my own bread and I have a garden and...." Chris shrugged and focused on measuring flour. "It makes me feel useful."

Bell didn't have anything to say right away, so he finished his brownie, washed it down with a swig of porter, and watched Chris melt butter in a saucepan. But he could only keep quiet for so long before he had to ask, "So. Do you often co-opt people into sorting out your business finances and then make them dinner? Or, uh, am I just special?"

Chris's shoulders tensed, and he was silent as he whisked flour into the melted butter in the pan. When he turned to open the refrigerator, he glanced at Bell, and his face was red. "I don't usually invite people over," he said. "Not even for accounting help. But—" Chris took the chicken from the fridge and began to dice it. He avoided Bell's gaze again.

"Hey," Bell said as he stood up.

Chris paused with his hand on the knife, then slowly set it down and met Bell's gaze.

"You can relax, if—I mean, this is a date, right?"

Chris lifted one corner of his mouth in a wry smile. "Yeah, Bell, it's a date."

Oh thank God.

Then Chris made a face at himself. "Though I really must be out of practice if my idea of a date involves help with accounts receivable."

"Well, I'm rusty too, so I appreciate the opportunity to show off. But yeah. You can relax. You're cute. You're funny. The whole home-cooked-meal thing raises the dating bar kind of a lot for me. So...." He took a step closer. "In case the flirting hasn't made it obvious, I'm pretty into the whole package."

Chris laughed, seemingly in spite of himself. "I have no idea why, but okay. If I get the dishes out, will you set the table? I'll put the potpies together and in the oven, and then if you want a tour, we can do that while they bake?"

Bell wouldn't mind a tour, but he was trying to work up the nerve for a kiss. All his courage seemed to have deserted him, though. Or maybe he'd used it up. "I'll make you a list later." Chris looked at him blankly. "Of all the reasons I…." Bell shrugged, less embarrassed and more unsure how to continue. *Like you. Am attracted to you. Want this to be a date.*

Chris acknowledged that with a shy lift of one shoulder. Then he turned back to the task at hand and the conversation lagged as the sound of cooking filled up the empty spaces.

Bell could have watched Chris roll out pie crust for hours. His shirtsleeves were pushed up, so Bell could ogle his forearms. But it was only a minute, maybe two, before Chris finished with the crust and turned to Bell. Bell could almost see him square his shoulders as he slipped his fingers into Bell's belt loops and tugged a bit. "I'm glad you're here," he said softly.

For a moment Bell thought for sure he'd get that kiss. "Me too," he admitted, no louder.

But then Chris smiled at him kind of dumbly, released his belt loops with a halfhearted swat to Bell's hip, and returned to his piecrust. "Just one minute to get these in the oven, and I'll give you that tour."

Bell's lips tingled for want of the kiss that almost was, and he watched Chris for a second, trying to figure him out. Something made him think *out of practice* didn't quite cover it, but it felt like it was too soon to ask.

Bell soon discovered Chris hadn't been kidding when he said the house was under construction. Though the kitchen had obviously made Chris's priority list, other parts of the house hadn't.

"It's kind of a long story, but this used to be my grandfather's house. He rented it out during the last years of his life, and the renter made some unauthorized updates, like stripping the carpet," Chris said, indicating the bare plywood in the rear sitting room. "But he didn't get around to installing the cheap laminate he bought. It's still in the basement. I should probably sell it on eBay or something." In the meantime the floor was bare, the walls furnished with paper that had once probably been stylish but had yellowed and begun to peel.

"The floor is cold," Bell commented, glad for the slippers.

"This part of the house is original, and there's nothing under this floor, so it can get chilly." Chris made a face. "I keep the doors closed in the winter and don't bother heating this part of the house unless I'm working in it. It should be better when I've reinsulated and laid a proper floor, but there's only so much I can do without sacrificing ceiling height."

A tiny hallway off the back sitting room led to two modest bedrooms with old-fashioned metal closet doors. Both rooms and closets were empty except for some boxes. The carpets were clean but not new, the walls recently painted neutral colors. Separating the bedrooms was a small, tidy bathroom with a toilet, tub/shower combo, and a tiny sink. Bottles of shampoo, conditioner, and bodywash lined the edge of the tub.

"I'm redoing the master bath," Chris explained. "That's why I've got all my stuff in here. I don't do plumbing work myself, so I'm at the mercy of someone else's schedule."

Bell wondered why he hadn't chosen one of the bedrooms back here, then, out of convenience. "Is this all original too?" The sink and the tub certainly looked like they could be antiques. Not in a bad way, though. Just like the truck, the fixtures had been well cared for.

Chris nodded. "Yeah. Grandpa couldn't afford a big house, but he tried to make up for it with quality, you know? He and Grandma were proud of what they had, and they took care of it."

The newer part of the house, which Chris said was an addition, was on the other side of the kitchen and told a slightly different story. The living room featured hardwood floors similar to those in Bell's apartment and a beautiful built-in entertainment unit that housed some of the ugliest knickknacks Bell had ever laid eyes on.

"I helped Grandpa build it when I was in high school." Chris smiled ruefully and ran his hand along one of the shelves. "I hated

Dad for volunteering me, but I'm glad he did. It kept me out of trouble and taught me a lot, you know?"

Bell shook his head. "Not really. Let's just say my parents aren't the hands-on type when it comes to this stuff." They were the "throw money at the problem until it goes away" type.

It turned out the rotted steps outside led into a tiled hallway that doubled as a laundry room.

The other door off the living room opened into the master bedroom, and suddenly Bell understood why Chris hadn't claimed one of the smaller bedrooms even temporarily. His bedroom furniture wouldn't have fit. An eight-and-a-half-foot-tall armoire stood in the corner, with a matching dresser in the same style and dark wood along the wall to its left. To its right—

"Um," Bell said as his mind filled with images that made his face turn hot. How many times was this going to happen to him? "Nice bed."

It reminded him of the one in his apartment, although the styling was different—smoother, rounder, and more elegant than the bold, square lines of Bell's bed. It looked just as sturdy and just as comfortable and, with Chris and the admission that this was a date behind him, just as suggestive, if not more so. Inviting, even.

Bell inhaled and turned around to catch Chris's eyes, licking his lips before he could quash the impulse. It had been a long time since he went out with a guy. What was the etiquette for asking if Chris put out on a first date?

Maybe he wouldn't have to. Chris was staring at his mouth, and an attractive flush bridged his nose and cheeks. Bell tried to make himself take a step forward, but before he could convince his feet to move, Chris broke eye contact and looked over Bell's shoulder at the bed. "Ah, thanks. My grandfather made it."

Okay, well, that killed the mood. Bell shook himself and tried to rally. "Oh. I wondered—I mean, did he make the one in my apartment too?"

Shaking his head, Chris took a step back into the living room, and Bell followed, unsure if he was disappointed or relieved. "No, uh… I did," he said, confirming Bell's earlier suspicion. "Back when I was still—and then it was too big to move."

Still what? Bell wondered, but then the timer went off in the kitchen and his stomach growled again, as if on cue.

Chris smiled and seemed to shake off whatever discomfort had come over him. Bell burned with curiosity, but he didn't want to push. "I'd better feed you before you waste away."

"Yes, please," Bell said as he took another step toward the kitchen. The savory scents of piecrust and creamy filling tickled his nose and made his mouth water.

The pie tasted as good as it smelled, and sitting at the little kitchen table with Chris felt comfortable. Cozy even. If seeing the bed had made him want to drag Chris down onto it and do all sorts of naked, sexy things, dinner made him want to cuddle on the couch under a warm fleece blanket. Bell mentally checked himself. It was one thing to want to jump a guy on the first date, but planning cozy, domestic evenings at home might be getting ahead of himself.

Nothing ventured, though, right? That was what his mother would have said, albeit under extremely different circumstances. So he slid his chair forward a few inches, until he could nudge Chris's foot with his—slippers and all.

Chris looked up, as obviously pleased as he was surprised, and nudged back. Maybe not as intimate as curling up together under a blanket, but Bell would take it.

"So where did you learn all these useful skills?" he asked and motioned to his plate. "I mean, cooking and gardening, that's one thing. But cooking and bread baking and woodworking and gardening? When do you sleep?"

Chris shrugged. "Idle hands and all that, I guess?" It was a little flip, and Bell would have let it go, but Chris continued. "Honestly I can get kind of, um… broody, I guess, sometimes. I love Pineville, but it's really quiet. Mix that with boredom, and I'm just a few steps too close to being the cranky dude in a rocking chair on his porch, scaring the local children."

"You'd have to rebuild the porch first," Bell said without thinking.

Chris gave him a look. "I'm not ready for the rocking chair either, smartass. I could probably cut down on my HGTV, though."

He should probably have his own show. Even if the dildo thing might have to air on HBO.

Bell shook his head. "Is there anything you don't do?"

Chris took a long drink of beer and then seemed to mull the question over a bit. "I can change a tire, but that's pretty much the extent of my car knowledge." He cleared his throat and turned the question back on Bell. "How about you, when you're not being an entrepreneurial genius?"

Bell opened his mouth to answer and then closed it again to think. Honestly he didn't know what he was good at anymore. But he didn't want to be a downer. He was okay with the fact that he was still figuring himself out. "Well, I can tie a knot in a cherry stem with my tongue," he said, which was true and, as a bonus, made Chris's ears turn red. "But I sort of quit my job to answer that question, I guess. I'll let you know when I figure it out."

"So you're not afraid to change things up, and you have enough drive to make things happen for yourself." Chris didn't make it sound like a question. "And you're diplomatic enough to get along with your family even when you're doing your own thing."

Now it was Bell's turn to go pink. It wasn't the sort of first-date compliment he was used to. Not that he could remember the last time a date had given him a compliment. "I mean, don't get me wrong. It takes a lot of restraint not to just tell Mom where to go sometimes." He smiled wanly and then grinned wider as something occurred to him. "Oh, hey. And I have a good sense of direction."

Chris laughed and trapped Bell's foot between his own. "Well, there you go. I can't even get on the highway going in the right direction without Google."

"And I have AAA, so you don't even have to get your hands dirty if we break down," Bell said. Now he was assuming they'd be taking road trips together. Oops.

But if Chris thought it was too soon for that, he didn't let on. "Perfect." He gestured at Bell's empty plate. "Seconds?"

Bell could have crushed another helping, but he didn't want to be uncomfortable later, in case the evening ended with more than a kiss. Too much heavy food before sex was a no-go. "It's delicious, but I saw how much butter you put in it. I'm good. Thanks, though."

Chris gave him an appraising look. "I'm sure you could easily handle a bit more."

Bell nearly snorted a mouthful of beer into his sinuses. He couldn't avoid the coughing fit, though, and Chris got up to thump him between the shoulder blades. When Bell looked up, Chris was holding back a laugh. "I probably could have phrased that better."

"I think you phrased it just fine," Bell replied before he could stop himself.

Unfortunately Chris didn't take the bait.

Bell didn't get it. He seemed interested. He said this was a date. Did Bell have something stuck between his teeth? Or did Chris just not put out on the first date? Was that weird? Had Bell just been kind of a slut last time he dated? Maybe he could ask the college kids next time they ordered a pizza.

Chris cleared his throat and gestured toward the living room. They left their plates where they were and relocated. "Anyway. You said something about writing copy for the Etsy shop?"

That was an interesting conversational segue. Bell looked sideways at Chris, who looked sincere. Bell could work with that, and surely if Chris had decided he wasn't interested, he would have gone for pretty much any topic of conversation that wasn't dildo related.

"Yeah. They look great, but we'll need something to go under the pictures. Luckily you can make anything sound good with the right copy."

Chris looked at him skeptically. "Is that right?"

"Granted, you have a good product, but I've been successful with much worse. Marketing classes aren't completely useless."

Bell looked around for a way to make his point. His eyes came to rest on the shelves of the entertainment unit and the knickknacks on them.

"Hmm," Bell said, moving closer. "This is an... unusual collection of small ceramic and textile objects, with a barnyard theme." He tipped his head to one side and scanned the shelves. "An eclectic selection that ranges from piglet napkin holders to hand-painted swan sugar bowls. There is something here for everyone." Bell glanced back to see Chris's reaction.

Chris was leaning forward, a sure sign of engagement, and rubbing his beard with a finger and thumb—another good sign and also kind of distracting.

Bell cleared his throat and continued. "For example, this specimen." Bell picked up a bull with a shiny red glaze and an odd, ridged texture. He'd grabbed it around the middle, so he also discovered, when his ring finger touched the underside, that the craftsman had made a good effort at anatomical realism.

Bell could hear Chris's soft snort as the bull went back to his spot on the shelf. Bell scanned the shelves and picked up a soft, moth-eaten gray donkey made from what smelled like unwashed sheep's wool. "This folk art piece is a charming representation of early twenty-first-century art fairs, at which handmade items were sold for exorbitant sums. Note the handmade ceramic hooves and eyes, which make this more than just your usual piece of ass."

Bell tried to keep a straight face, but Chris burst into laughter. Bell lost his composure too, and they both cracked up almost to the point of tears. Bell clutched the little donkey against his chest. When he caught his breath, he grinned at Chris. "Sold? Or do you need more convincing?"

Chris wiped at his eyes with the back of his hand. "One more?"

Bell was pretty sure that Chris hadn't smiled that easily over the past few days, and he turned back to the entertainment center, determined to coax even more laughter from him. In the very middle of the display, Bell spotted the collection's prize. "Here we have the pièce de résistance of this unique group: a proud cock decorated with multiple cheerful colors reminiscent of rainbow sherbet—hold up a second." He turned to Chris. "Seriously. What's the deal here?"

He hadn't known Chris long, but he would have bet the contents of his wallet that Chris wasn't the big pastel ceramic rooster kind of guy. Until a few minutes before, Bell would have denied such a person existed. He held up the evidence.

Chris shrugged, looking both embarrassed and resigned. "Would you believe they belonged to my ex?"

Bell had apparently just blundered into The Exes Conversation. Oops. "Well, clearly they don't belong to you," Bell said. "I mean, you have actual good taste." He put the donkey back on the shelf and came to sit next to Chris. "Look, I'm not going to pry about your weird ex situation—and I mean your ex is weird, not so much that you have a weird situation. But *dude*. Those shelves have under lighting, like in a museum of kitsch."

Chris flushed pink, but he nodded. "The lighting was Derek's idea. It looks like hell with the cords all over the place, but I wasn't going to drill into Grandpa's entertainment center for weird, shadowy lighting for yard-sale stuff. Besides"—Chris shrugged—"this isn't the swanky mountain home he expected, and I wasn't bringing a banker's salary home anymore."

Wait a second. *"Banker's salary?"* Bell was probably gawping. He looked at Chris, who seemed relaxed and casual among the things he'd made or fixed with his hands. Bell tried to picture him in a gray suit and tie, seated in a glass-walled office, but the image wouldn't stick in his head.

"I'm smarter than I look?" Chris said it as though it were a question.

"No," Bell protested and then realized how that sounded. "Yes," he said, which sounded worse. He felt his cheeks flame. "Is this a trick question?"

"I'm not sure," Chris said. "You seemed surprised."

"You're definitely smart enough, but—" Bell sat up and gave Chris a stern look. "Did you really need help with your invoices, or was that a ploy?"

Chris rubbed a hand through his hair and grinned sheepishly. "I don't keep up with it until I'm looking for something specific, and then it takes a whole day. It's not like I don't know *how*. I was just working with a lot more zeros than I do now."

Bell sat back on the sofa and shook his head. "I've been tricked into viewing disturbing barnyard ceramics by a nefarious banker." He chuckled at his own joke, but it turned into a yawn, and Bell slapped his hand over his mouth. "I'm so sorry. I promise I'm not bored."

Chris patted him on the arm and squeezed a little. "No offense taken. I put you to work and then plied you with beer and hot food and brownies. It's probably past time I got you home."

Part of Bell really wanted to protest, to tell Chris he didn't have a curfew, but he liked Chris too much to fuck it up by coming on too strong or overstaying his welcome.

"Sure. Another busy day in the furniture business tomorrow." Bell stood up and stretched. If his tee lifted up a bit to show a sliver of skin, well, he wasn't bothered. He glanced down at Chris, whose gaze immediately darted away from Bell's midriff. Nope. Not bothered at all.

"Come on." He gave Chris a hand to pull him up. "Wouldn't want you to keep me out on the wild streets of Pineville so late."

Chris laughed as he bent to put on his shoes. "At least there was chicken potpie?"

"It was delicious. The company wasn't bad either." Bell lowered his voice to a whisper as Chris opened the door and stepped out. "I'm apparently the kind of bookkeeper that can be bought."

Chris's eyes reflected the kitchen light as he looked back at Bell from a few steps down. "I guess I'll have to keep that in mind. I can provide dinners—"

"Or breakfast?"

Chris coughed, and Bell imagined he'd gone red again, though in the darkness, he couldn't see. Bell wondered how long it had been since Chris made someone breakfast. "It's been known to happen, from time to time," Chris allowed. He was still smiling, but it seemed different. Bell had pushed too hard again, he thought. "Not for a while, though." Bell almost expected him to add "Not tomorrow either," but he didn't.

They got in the truck, and Bell turned slightly toward Chris, leaned forward, and then stopped himself. Maybe Chris just needed Bell to go out on a limb first. He could work with that. "Full disclosure, okay?" Chris nodded, so Bell plunged on. "Not seeing anyone, no homicidal exes in the past, but I've been basically dating work for the past couple of years."

"I did get that impression," Chris admitted as he started the truck and the tense set of his shoulders relaxed. In the glow of the dashboard light, the lines around his mouth softened too, until they disappeared. "Me too, as I'm sure you've guessed."

Bell nodded and tried not to be disappointed that Chris didn't offer more. "Yeah, so. I can't remember the last time I had good sex, and I'm constantly restraining myself from jumping you. But uh... I get the impression you're not the falling-into-bed type, and that's cool."

Chris's shoulders tightened again, and he dropped his gaze to his hands. "Depends on what you call 'good,' I suppose," he said. "It's been a while. Might be overselling myself a bit."

Oh. The situation could be worse than he'd feared. "Hey." Bell put his hand on Chris's knee. "I like you, okay? No pressure here. I just want to get in at the front of the line before the men of Pineville realize who they've let get away."

"I'm not sure there are any single gay men in Pineville."

Not for much longer, anyway, Bell hoped.

Chris pulled the truck to a stop in front of the shop.

"Well, best not to take chances, right?" Bell said.

"Didn't realize you had such a conservative attitude," Chris said, smile lines crinkling around his eyes.

"Get in early and hold on," Bell said, with as serious an expression as he could manage, given how badly he wanted to get his hands into Chris's hair.

Chris snorted and opened the truck door. "Come on, let's get you inside before Jenny takes pictures of us from across the street."

It was Jenny's day off, but Bell didn't correct him. He was getting the full gentleman treatment. He wasn't sure anyone had ever walked him to his apartment before, at least not without the expectation that he'd invite them in and spread his legs for them. He hopped out of the truck and closed the door just as Chris came around the front.

"Oh," Chris said. "I was going to get the door for you."

Bell could see his flush even in the yellowish light from the streetlamp. "An old-fashioned kind of boy?"

Bell meant it as a gentle tease, but Chris nodded. "You've only been here a week, but I don't think I've got many surprises left for you to figure out."

Bell stepped closer and slid his hand into the bend of Chris's elbow. "Nothing wrong with being who you really are," he said, tugging Chris to his side. "That's a better surprise than most I've gotten."

"Well," Chris started, and he was obviously never going to stop talking and get a clue, so Bell put one hand behind Chris's neck and silenced him with a kiss.

If Chris was surprised, he didn't show it. He made a low, pleased hum that vibrated against Bell's mouth, and he rested his hands on Bell's hips and teased his thumbs over Bell's hipbones. The warmth of his hands made Bell shiver and press closer. He should've brought a jacket—but then he wouldn't be able to feel the heat of Chris's chest. Chris nipped gently at Bell's lower lip as he slid his hands under Bell's shirt. Bell could feel the rough skin scratching along his sides, and he twitched without meaning to.

"Ticklish?" Chris smiled against his mouth. "Useful to know."

Bell winced as he pulled back a bit. "I'm not sure I wanted you to know that," he said.

"Too late," Chris said and kissed Bell again. Then he pulled his hands back and straightened Bell's shirt. "May I walk you to your door?"

Bell frowned. "My door is a whole six yards away, Chris."

Chris shrugged. "Lot of driveway crime in Pineville. Wouldn't want my date to trip over a cat or something before he got home safely."

"My hero," Bell said, feigning a swoon. Then he tugged Chris forward by the hand. Maybe he'd get lucky after all.

Chris's true game became apparent when they reached the landing at the top of the stairs and Chris maneuvered Bell to lean his back against the door. This time his grip didn't tickle when he put his hands on Bell's sides, and when Chris kissed him, Bell appreciated having something to support his weight. Chris's lips were soft and so was his beard, but when he licked into Bell's mouth, the gentleness ended. Bell tilted his head and hooked his fingers into Chris's waistband. His breath hitched as Chris teased Bell's lower lip with his tongue and then scraped it with his teeth.

Bell gasped and pressed himself against Chris. He slid one hand into the soft hair at the base of Chris's skull and let a few strands slip between his fingers so he could tug at them a little. Chris responded by pushing Bell back against the door. With just a little maneuvering, Bell could have slotted his leg between Chris's thighs.

Before he could gather himself to try it, though, Chris backed off, and the kiss turned into as much of a tease as the rest of the evening. Quick, erotic flirts of Chris's tongue over Bell's lips left him light-headed and hard enough to cause a scene in public. It took him several seconds to notice when Chris stopped kissing him. He was too busy making sure his knees still worked.

He opened his eyes to look at Chris, who was flushed and gorgeous, even—or maybe especially—with his glasses askew. Bell nuzzled into Chris's neck, mostly for the beard, but also so he wouldn't pant onto Chris's face. "Wow," he murmured.

"I've been wanting to do that all day," Chris confessed, idly soothing his hands down Bell's back.

"I've been waiting for you to do that all day," Bell said. "No need to hold back on my account. Feel free."

Chris drew back slowly and rubbed his scruff gently against the side of Bell's face, until he was far enough away for Bell to see his grin. Bell was going to need a moisturizer with aloe, but it would be worth it. Chris quickly kissed him on the lips again and then stepped away so they weren't touching from shoulders to knees anymore.

Bell frowned. "Like I said, no need to hold back."

"It's late," Chris said, but he sounded rueful.

Bell wanted to protest or, better yet, kiss him again, but if Chris was tired, maybe he shouldn't.

"And I'm supposed to measure the Joneses' dining room tomorrow at eight, to get the right size for their set."

It was such a responsible-sounding excuse that Bell again remembered he hadn't dated anyone since he was a student. Maybe dating in the adult world didn't work the way it did on TV. "Okay, Mr. Responsible," he said, shaking his head. "Kiss me like that and then leave me at the door. We'll have to save the wild monkey sex for another time."

Chris choked on his own breath, and his eyebrows went up. "I hate to disappoint," he gasped out. For a moment Bell thought he might reconsider going home, but then Chris added with a sly smile, "It's a shame you don't have marketing work to keep you busy and distracted."

"I'll be up all night either way." *Seriously, please come in.* But nothing doing. Finally Bell gave up on his dream of getting laid tonight and planted one more quick kiss on Chris's cheek. "Thanks for dinner," he said. Then he winked. "Let me know if you ever want to do that breakfast."

Chris groaned theatrically. "You're terrible." He leaned in again, and Bell was mentally fist-pumping and preparing for Jell-O legs, but Chris just pecked him on the cheek. His beard tickled the soft skin. "Will I see you around the shop tomorrow?"

"I might be busy doing market research," Bell said. "I have a lot to learn about wood, apparently."

Chris snorted and shook his head. Bell could tell he was fighting a grin, though. "And I'm sure you're going to ask me to teach you?"

"Well, if it doesn't interfere with the Joneses' furniture."

"I think I can squeeze in a crash course in wood. I really do have to go, though."

Bell sighed and pouted for effect. "Fine."

"You have to let go of my belt loops."

Whoops. "Guess you're not the only one who needs to go to bed."

Chris didn't say anything, just raised an eyebrow until Bell let go. Chris caught one of his hands and gave it a brief squeeze. "Good night, Bell." Then he turned and walked down the stairs.

Bell slumped back against the door and stayed there as he listened to Chris let himself out, start up his truck, and drive away.

There was no way he was going to be able to fall asleep. He'd play tonight's events over and over in his brain until it melted and leaked out his ears—if he didn't give in and hump his mattress out of sheer frustration.

That actually sounded appealing. At least until Bell remembered he lived with a stockpile of artisanal dildos and should really familiarize himself with the product if he was going to hawk it. Hey, you only live once.

Optimistically he'd left lube and condoms in the bedside table when he unpacked. Which meant his first step was….

Bell pried the lid off the Rubbermaid container. *Pick a card, any card.* His dick was already half-hard in his jeans, or he might have spent more time choosing. He knew more or less what he wanted— something long enough, with an embellishment to provide texture. It didn't have to be pretty.

It was, though, when he spied the one he wanted. It was made from different shades of gold wood and had an intriguing bulb at the tip. They were all pretty. But that one called to him, and he wasn't going to paw through the whole bin. He picked it up, and the solid weight and firm smoothness of it surprised him.

Okay. He was going to do this.

Bell kicked off his jeans, wormed out of his shirt, and lay down on the bed. He gave his half-hard dick a light squeeze and hissed at the slightly rough, dry pressure. Chris's hands would be rough too, probably, calloused and capable. But he was too careful to jerk Bell off like this for long. He'd definitely….

Bell reached for the lube and poured himself a palmful. The slow slide of his hand made heat blossom in his stomach and tension coil in his balls, and his nipples tightened But it wasn't enough.

He couldn't shake the fantasy of Chris leaving that bin for him on purpose. What if Bell had opened the bedside table drawer and found the dildo he'd chosen inside?

He slid his hand lower and smeared lube over his hole. It had been a while since he'd done it, but one finger slid in easily, two with hardly any more trouble. He sighed into the stretch and leaned his head back against the mattress as he stroked the fingers of his other hand over his erection, keeping his touch light.

The dildo he'd chosen was thick enough to be enticing and curved slightly. Bell's tongue slipped out to lick at his bottom lip as he thought about the rounded bulb at the tip, just wide enough to make his lips stretch around it if he took it into his mouth.

He swallowed and his mouth watered, just a little, at the fantasy, and suddenly he couldn't wait any longer. He hadn't looked up what sort of lube one might use with wooden dildos, but that was what condoms were for. He rolled one down the length of the toy and slicked it up. And then—

He closed his eyes and let the fantasy take over.

He shivered when he imagined someone—Chris—pressing the wooden toy against him. He pictured Chris kneeling between Bell's parted thighs, drizzling a stream of slick down the shaft of the carved dildo to get it ready. Bell would—he would spread his legs wider, angle himself better, make it clear that he wanted it, that he wanted Chris to fuck him with the toy he'd carved with his own strong hands, that he'd shaped just right for Bell.

Bell caught his bottom lip between his teeth just as he swiped his thumb over the head of his cock, spread his own slickness around, and pushed the toy inside. The lack of handle made it a little challenging to find the right angle, but Bell persevered, and he bit back a cry as the tip of the toy nudged his prostate. It had been so long since anyone had touched him or since he'd had the energy to touch himself that he knew he wouldn't last long.

Chris might draw it out and tease Bell until he begged for it. But Bell didn't have the patience. He thrust the toy with intent, fisted his cock with his other hand, and imagined Chris watching him, Chris touching him, Chris fucking inside him until his eyes rolled back in his head. Then he came, groaning out incoherent moans of encouragement to his imaginary partner.

CHAPTER SIX

BELL SLEPT like the dead and woke up feeling both well rested and, if not sore, slightly used. He looked at the dildo resting on the towel on the nightstand. "Well, that's one satisfied customer," he said out loud. Then it occurred to him—he'd pretty much put that piece of merchandise squarely in the "used, no returns accepted" category. He could definitely write an enthusiastic testimonial. But maybe after he had a shower.

Bell had just about worked up the energy to head to the bathroom when his phone rang with his brother's ringtone. It was weird for Cam to call so early, but when Bell looked at the screen, it read *Cameron— Work*. That actually made more sense, which said a lot about Bell's brother. Calling from home so early on a Saturday would mean an emergency. Calling from the office was just Cam taking a break.

"Hey, bro. Up with the birds?"

"The sun is up, come on," Cam said. "Plenty of time yet to finish this draft, dictate a couple of letters, and maybe relax with a copy of the minutes from the meeting of the board of directors." He laughed, but he didn't sound particularly chipper, so Bell tried to lighten his mood in his time-tested little-brother way.

"Board meeting. Wow. You know how to have a good time. You know all the lawyers from TV would be getting dressed up to go to some fancy brunch hotspot with the beautiful and dangerous people. Sexy."

Cam snorted. "That's the litigators. We in-house types do all of the work with zero sex appeal."

Once upon a time, Bell thought Cam's job was sexy. He was a sophomore in college when Cam landed the job on the in-house-counsel team for a big department-store chain. Bell went to see him his first week in his office on the thirtieth floor of a glass skyscraper just across the street from the fancy flagship store. Everything was black leather, dark wood, or glass. A severely handsome guy about Bell's age had brought him coffee in a tiny cup, and an equally intimidating beautiful girl showed him into Cam's office. At the time Bell was filled with a combination of envy and desire to have the same gig with the same perks. Now, flopped on his bed and covered in a handmade quilt while a big orange cat snoozed on his feet, Bell could barely imagine tolerating that life for a single day, much less imagine a life that mandated an office appearance on Saturday mornings.

"So is that why you're calling me from work so early? Thought maybe someone in Pineville could help you spice up your routine?" He made himself laugh, which jostled Lady Frances. She glared at him before settling down again.

Cam hissed like he was sucking air through his teeth. "Sorry, man. You weren't still asleep, were you?"

Bell wasn't going to tell his brother what he'd been doing just before he called. He cleared his throat. "No, I was up. You know how it is in flyover country. Early to bed, early to rise." Bell had to swallow a snort at the unintended innuendo. "I was just about to put the coffee on. Besides, always good to talk to you, you know, even if this probably isn't just a social call."

"No, it's not, I'll have Sh—oh, damn, I can't believe I did that," Cam groaned. "I nearly said I'd have Sharon set one of those up for you. Ugh."

Bell loved his brother, but he *definitely* wasn't jealous of his job. "You held back, so there's still some real human left in you."

"Ha-ha. Seriously. I needed to ask you about that girl you knew at college, the one who painted the murals. You still know her?"

"Lydia? Yeah, I have her number. Your office need a new look?" Bell imagined Lydia in her paint-splattered overalls putting a bright, cheerful mural on Cam's office wall. Maybe chattering monkeys. That sounded like it might be a good addition.

"No, it's for Mandy's room. Monica thought we should give her a little 'big sister' present before the baby comes—something to go with the theme of her room."

Bell thought the idea of a big sibling present was cute, but he figured a book or a toy or maybe a cute outfit might do the trick. Trust Cam and Monica to come up with something as extravagant as a custom-painted mural. "So you're going for the animal sidekick thing?"

"Yeah, the whole Disney zoo. You know, Flower, Pumbaa, that reindeer from *Frozen*—"

"Sven," Bell supplied. God, how did Cam not know that? Mandy made Bell watch that movie at least half-a-dozen times, and he was just her overworked uncle.

"Yeah, him. All the ones from her DVDs."

"That's nice," Bell said. "I'll e-mail you Lydia's info in a bit."

"Thanks, dude. Look, I know we haven't talked much since you moved, but work has been so busy and, you know, the baby coming, and—"

"Cam. It's cool." The last thing Bell wanted was for his brother to feel like he had any other obligations. Bell wouldn't be surprised if he added "weekly check-in, younger brother" to his calendar.

"I'll probably be able to get away for Thanksgiving, so we can catch up then, okay?"

Bell suppressed a groan. He wasn't ready to think about the holidays. Luckily for him Cameron's landline rang in the background.

"Damn. It's the Miami office. Gotta take it. I'll talk to you soon. Take care, bro."

The call dropped, and Bell shook his head. He was amazed Cam seemed to be holding up so well. More power to him.

Bell spent the morning working lazily in a clean pair of pajama pants and a T-shirt from his old fraternity. He'd never had a job he could work from home before. This was even better than the jeans and polo shirt he wore delivering pizza.

He picked website colors, font, and layout, and wrote some basic advertising copy, but while he got a lot done, he didn't know much about the woods Chris used. He could make a guess at what might be oak or cherry, but it would probably be a pretty bad guess, so he'd just end up doing it over. He held up one curved, slender dildo that was deep reddish brown with a grain that was, well, *pretty*. But hell if he knew the proper way to describe it.

He checked the time. Just after noon. Chris would be back from measuring the Joneses' dining room. Maybe they could do lunch and Chris could look over Bell's product review.

Bell swapped his pajama pants for a pair of holey jeans. Then he toed on his shoes, grabbed his keys, and headed for the door. He could hear Chris's voice, so he peeked into the woodshop. Chris was on the phone with his back to Bell, but he half turned to give a smile and a wave as he nodded along with whatever the caller was saying. It gave Bell a few moments to think about what the protocol was here. After one date, what was appropriate? A nod and a smile? A brief hug? A confession of a spectacular fantasy and masturbation session?

Bell looked for a flat, bare surface on which to put his computer but then reconsidered. Sawdust coated everything like snow on Santa's workshop. Best leave the sensitive electronics in the office.

"Okay. No, the armoire should be finished before then, no problem. I'll arrange delivery for that week." Chris paused. "Yes, I can schedule a Saturday delivery."

Chris gestured with his mug to indicate there was coffee if Bell was interested. Bell smiled to see a clean mug already waiting. It was like Chris wanted, even expected, Bell to come down and hang out when he got up. He shifted his computer bag to one shoulder and poured himself a mug, inhaling deeply as Chris finished up his phone call.

"Hey," Chris said. "Did you have a good night?"

Not "Did you sleep well?" but "Did you have a good night?" As though he knew exactly what Bell had gotten up to the night before. Well, maybe he did. It wouldn't be hard to guess.

"I mean, it could've been better," Bell said, batting his eyelashes, and Chris snorted a laugh.

"I apologize if it didn't include enough barnyard curios." Chris raised an eyebrow. "Though maybe, if we knew something about shopping on the Internet, we might be able to fill that ho—need." Chris made a very prompt recovery, but not before Bell realized where that sentence had been going. He badly wanted to respond to what Chris was undoubtedly thinking, but he took a deep, too-hot gulp of coffee instead.

"Funny you should mention Internet commerce."

"Funny ha-ha?"

"Funny as in 'what a coincidence.'" Bell nodded at the bag hanging over his shoulder. "While you've been playing with your power tools, I've been working."

"I haven't even gotten to drill anything yet today," Chris protested, eyes wide with innocence. "Too busy measuring."

Bell wasn't touching that. "Do you want to see what I've been working on?" he asked. He headed toward the front of the shop, where he could safely set down his computer. Then he thought better of it and asked, "Any teenage girls hiding in the wings?"

"You can relax." Chris laughed and covered his eyes with one hand as Bell opened his laptop. "Chloe's working a booth at the flea market for me. God. If Grandpa could see me now."

Bell paused with his finger on the trackpad. "Wait. Is he the one who named the store Good Wood?"

"No, that was me." Chris took Joseph's usual seat behind the front desk and hooked his foot on the metal bar under the stool. "It made sense to change the name. Grandpa did business as McGregor's. Made it kind of hard for people to find him, you know? I have his tools and work ethic, but I moved and changed the name and... he'd have understood. Hell, he'd have done it himself if he thought of it. But probably not the, uh, adult novelty part."

"You might be surprised. Granted Etsy has made selling these things much easier, but I was kind of impressed at how long people have been doing this sort of thing." When Chris raised an eyebrow, Bell amended, "I meant making sex toys out of natural materials, specifically. Not, uh… you know, general…." He made a gesture that got the point across without being too crass or too suggestive. "Like wood, and ivory back in the day, ceramic and stone…."

He glanced up to see Chris trying not to laugh. "Are you mocking my market research?"

"No, no, just appreciating your passion for the subject." Chris nodded to the screen. "So, are you gonna let me see it or keep me guessing?"

"Thought you'd never ask." Bell pulled up the page. "Ta-da! Or, well, sort of ta-da. A few little holes still need filling—don't." He groaned as Chris grinned unrepentantly. Then he sighed and started again. "I had to insert some filler text because I don't actually know anything about woods or wood grain or medical-grade varnish or whatever."

Chris peered at the text on the screen. "Well, you got that one right." He pointed at an entry. "The deep reddish brown wood that is reminiscent of cherries is, in fact, cherry. Well done."

Bell felt his cheeks pink up at the compliment. He was so doomed. "Lucky guess," he said. "I thought it was really pretty, the color and the way it"—*curved like it would hit your sweet spot just right until you cried*—"looked like it could be some sort of pretty, decorative thing for the living room."

"That would be awesome," Chris said, his voice taking on a wistful quality. "Displaying a handmade dildo on your coffee table like it were an expensive piece of art, daring your visitors to comment. That's quality trolling right there."

"Oh sure," Bell agreed. "But I don't think I want to know what my mom would say."

Though he knew exactly what his mom would say, because she'd essentially already said it.

"Are you thinking of sending a link to the shop to your mom?"

"I don't think she needs another shock like that." Bell rolled his eyes.

"Another shock?" Chris's forehead creased in concern. "Bell, is she not cool with you being—"

Oh God. Bell had given him the wrong idea. He shook his head. "With me being gay? No. She's fine with that."

"So, other skeletons in the family closet?"

"Skeletons, collections of woodcuts of Victorian ladies spanking each other." Bell shrugged. "What's the difference?"

"Well, there's a slightly different audience for those it appeals to, for one," Chris said. "I hope, anyway. Whose woodcuts?"

Bell sighed. "Mom's uncle. Seemed like a perfectly normal old rich guy until he died and his will stipulated his 'antique craftsmanship assortment' should be donated to the British Museum."

"You're joking."

"I don't joke about the Bellamy Collection."

"The Bellamy Collection?"

"Rutherford K. Bellamy. He was old and rich, so Mom thought naming her youngest after him might be a good way to curry favor. Little did she know that the piles of cash were earmarked for charity and that he'd shame the family when the papers wrote about the extensive collection of nineteenth-century porn that he donated."

Bell couldn't tell if Chris was trying not to laugh or if he was getting upset on Bell's behalf. "How old were you when he passed away?"

"About twelve, I think?"

"What did your parents tell you about him?"

Bell shrugged and wondered where this line of questioning was headed. "The truth. I don't know if they thought I'd be disappointed not to get an inheritance or what, but my mom explained what he'd done with his money and that she was upset about him donating—I forget how she put it, exactly. 'Lewd images of women,' or something. I'm sure she meant to explain that it was the publicity that bothered her, but I thought she thought I'd be upset not to get the collection, so I tried to reassure her." Bell waited for understanding to dawn on Chris's face.

"Oh, you didn't."

Bell shook his head ruefully. "Oh yeah. 'It's okay, Mom. I'm gay anyway.'"

"I'm sure that was an immense relief, knowing that her adolescent son wasn't interested in naked ladies."

"She was actually really fine with it. Of course then she made sure, at every available opportunity, that I only met the right *sort* of boy. As soon as I was old enough, she pulled strings to get me a job at the country club. I know she thought tennis was a proper activity, but I don't think she ever caught the irony of pushing me to be a ball boy." Bell smirked. "Or the amazing opportunities for mischief there were at Ainsley Valley."

"Well, parents don't have to know everything."

"Probably better they don't," Bell agreed, wondering what his mother would make of Chris. Well, *she* wasn't dating him, so she could keep her opinions to herself. "What about you? Did your parents freak? I guess your grandfather took it okay."

"They didn't always understand, but they always loved me and tried to be supportive." Chris picked up a pen from the carved wooden holder and doodled on the edge of the calendar. He probably needed something to do with his hands while he talked. "They were a little older when they had me and also not very worldly. So when I came out to them, they were expecting something like *Some Like It Hot*, that I was going to be dressing in women's clothes and basically being a musical theater cliché. Not that there's anything wrong with that," he added hastily. "But that wasn't me."

"Fortunately flannel really works for you," Bell said without a trace of sarcasm.

"Hey now," Chris said, mock seriously. "This is a work environment."

"Oh, sorry." Bell blinked. "Flannel really works for you, *sir*."

Chris swatted at him. "Brat." Then he shook his head and went back to his story. "When they retired, they bought a trailer in Utah. God knows why. So I don't see them very much, but it's not weird or anything. My mom calls once a week or so."

"My mom calls once a week too, but our conversations are probably different." Bell couldn't imagine his mother setting foot in a trailer, never mind buying one. "Anyway, back to the task at hand."

Oops.

Chris gave him a wry look but let it slide. "The page looks good. General shop info, specific product info—testimonials?"

Bell reached over and tapped at the laptop. "Here's a sample testimonial—tell me what you think." He resisted the urge to fidget. "I'm going to refill my coffee. Want yours topped up?"

Chris grunted his assent and held out his mug as he stared at the screen.

Bell didn't hurry to refill their mugs and made a game out of how slowly he could pour the milk. Chris didn't know it yet, but he was getting a very honest and thorough review. When Bell heard a faint half mutter, half sigh from the counter, he dared to return.

He set the mugs down at the end of the counter. Chris immediately wrapped both hands around his. His skin had gone pink under his beard, and it seemed like he didn't want to look at anything but the screen.

"So," Bell said after a few seconds, "what did you think?"

Chris took a deep breath. "It's certainly vivid. I didn't know there were templates for sex toy reviews, but…." His next words tumbled out atop each other. "I'm pretty sure I know which one this is about."

Templates? Bell was nearly offended, as though Chris had accused him of plagiarizing his sincere and well-considered dildo review. "Um, as far as I know, there aren't. Templates, I mean."

Chris looked at him with dawning astonishment… or maybe horror. Still, in for a penny, in for a pound.

"It's pretty cool, though, that you can tell which one it is. The one with the pale and deep gold contrast and the bulb on the end, right?"

"Yes," Chris said slowly. "I was thinking about making that one with a handle, if we were going to offer specific models."

Bell's jaw dropped. "You're taking this seriously?"

Chris frowned. "Of course I am. It's a good idea—*you* have good ideas, some of which are in this review, and I'll get over wondering what my mom would think soon enough." He raised a shoulder in a half shrug. "And you managed to write a really vivid description, so whatever else your last job did, they managed to train you to describe anything, no matter what. What?"

Bell was shaking his head. "That wasn't just marketing BS." Bell reached into his pocket to retrieve his wallet and pulled out a few twenties, which he thrust at Chris.

"What's that for?"

Bell sighed, dropped the money on the counter, and nudged it toward Chris. "I think we need a 'you test it, you buy it' policy, so I'm buying it."

Chris picked up the money and counted it, then held two of the bills toward Bell. "You gave me eighty bucks. I wouldn't charge more than forty for some shop waste and ten minutes on the lathe."

Good grief. "And *that* is why you need a damn consultant."

"I don't disagree, but I still don't think it's worth eighty dollars," Chris protested.

Bell crossed his arms over his chest and glared. Damn, Chris was actually not getting it. "It. Was. Worth. Every. Penny," Bell said, smiling like a shark. "Plus I took the employee discount. You're actually charging $110."

"I am?" Chris looked at Bell and sighed. "You're the marketing guy, so I guess you've done your research." Chris was quiet for a moment and then began to laugh. "We're going to be dildo millionaires, huh?"

"Pretty much," Bell said. They wouldn't really, but it was a fun thought. "There are worse ways to earn a house on the beach with a cabana boy."

"Much worse. Though if we're going to get rich, I better make sure we have enough inventory."

Bell leaned back so he could look through the doorway to the woodshop. There were scraps everywhere, bits and pieces of wood on almost every horizontal surface. If the first time he'd walked in, it looked sloppy, now it looked like a treasure trove of different colors and shapes waiting to be made into dildos.

His libido seriously needed to chill. If he was going to start getting hard every time he saw a pile of wood scraps, it was going to be a problem.

Chris got up from the counter and came up behind Bell. "Pretty much anything that isn't leaning against the wall is fair game for new product," he said. "I've been throwing anything too small for furniture but big enough for something else into that plywood bin behind the band saw."

Bell looked over his shoulder and rolled his eyes. "Big enough to be a sex toy—you should probably get used to saying it in a business context. I'm going to put Artisan Dildo Maker on your next tax return."

"You're a terrible influence," Chris said. "Go do some marketing while I find the other bins of dildo inventory."

"Got it, chief." Bell took his laptop and coffee to a comfy chair shoved in a corner. He put his feet up on a crate and got into a comfortable slouch that he always felt was his best working posture. He brought up the other tabs in his browser, one of which showed the new message icon on his e-mail.

The message had the informative subject "Hi," so it was probably spam, but Bell clicked into it anyway.

Hi Bell, I'm a specialty recruiter and I got your name from a friend. I understand you're looking for a new position in a boutique consulting group, & what I know about your background makes me think we should talk. It would be 60% travel & work from home the rest of the time. I'll be in Pineville next week to do some recruiting at the college—lunch?

It was signed "DJ." The e-mail address didn't show a last name.

The second new e-mail was from his mom. *Hi, sweetheart! I'm glad you're settling in. I know you said you're doing a few things, but I hope you don't mind I passed your name on to a recruiter that Elaine Zimmerman knows. He'll reach out to you soon. Elaine says he's made some very good placements!*

Bell rolled his eyes. That was typical Mom, offering congratulations and a show of support only to follow it with a suggestion of what he could be doing better. On the plus side, he didn't have to worry about this DJ person being a creep or an axe murderer or a phishing scam.

Still, he wasn't going to answer right now. It was Saturday. Bell was over the life where he worked seven days a week.

Unless it involved his cute property-manager-maybe-boyfriend's artisan-dildo Etsy shop, apparently.

Thump.

Bell looked up just in time to catch a glimpse of sparse red chest hair through the open top buttons of Chris's plaid shirt as he set down another giant blue Rubbermaid container. Bell looked at Chris and then at the blue bin. It had sounded heavy.

He couldn't help it. He just blurted it out. "Have you been sexually frustrated, by any chance?"

Chris's face reddened. Bell was trying to stammer an apology when Chris shrugged and held out his hands in a self-deprecating gesture. "Oddly enough the men of Pineville haven't been lining up to get a piece of aging carpenter, so I've had some free time on my hands."

Bell didn't know whether to be grateful that the men of Pineville were too straight, too blind, or too stupid to appreciate Chris, or to be angry at whoever made him describe himself in that way. "More like 'sexy artisan who's ruggedly handsome and great with his hands,'" Bell said and quickly added, "Not that you need to put that in a personal ad."

"And why not?"

"That model is off the market," Bell said primly.

"Oh, well." Chris shook his head, but Bell could tell he was pleased. "Here I thought it was us only children who had trouble with sharing."

"We can be bad at it together." Bell toed the Rubbermaid container. "So show me the goods."

Chris pried the lid off. Bell watched attentively, because Chris wasn't the only sexually frustrated man in the room, and Bell was not above trying to look down his shirt. They took stock of the box. Metaphorically. The actual stock taking they'd do with a tape measure, spreadsheet, and camera.

Bell took a long look, though he resisted the urge to just dig his hands in. He suddenly recalled that his mother used to say "Look with your eyes, not with your hands" every time they went into a fancy shop when he was a kid. It made him giggle, and he wondered what Chris would do if he just stuck two grabby hands into the bin. The wood would probably feel smooth and cool, but Bell let his better angels prevail.

The contents displayed a surprising variety of shapes, colors, and sizes. "That's quite a selection you have there. Inventory might take a while."

"This is a few years' worth of work," Chris said. "And not all of them are worth selling, probably. I was just screwing around."

"Screwing around so other people can screw themselves," Bell said philosophically. "Hey, what do you think about custom orders? Like, say someone wants this dildo"—he pointed at a short, thick one with multiple ridges—"in a different wood?"

Chris shook his head. "This is a side gig. Commissions like that will take up too much time, and if I have to special order something in, I'll have to hike the prices. So no, for now."

Bell nodded and typed a note. "Okay, no custom dickery."

Chris snorted.

"The next thing is names."

"Names?" Chris sounded dubious.

"Yeah, here. Hand me one." Bell held out his hand until Chris got with the program and put a short, thick piece in it. "We have a few choices. We can go the simple but very boring route of calling them by number. Or we can give them names like Brown Beauty or use actual names like Dave."

"You want to name a hundred-odd sex toys."

"Marketing," Bell said knowingly. "Who are we appealing to here? People who want the discretion of a number, or people who want the fun whimsy of buying something called the Conductor to fuck themselves with?" He pointed to another dildo, this one slender, made of dark wood with a white tip.

"So yes, you want to name a hundred-odd dildos."

"We don't have to call any of them Dave. I have an ex named Dave, actually. I definitely wouldn't buy a dildo named Dave. So maybe no people names."

"I agree," Chris said.

"Fair enough. If you want to go for a classy, discreet feel, how about Maple Curves or Birch Ridges?"

Chris appeared to relax at the suggestion.

"So although we run the risk of sounding like a subdivision or a golf club with Alder Slopes, we can also get a bit cheeky with something like Cherry Plug," Bell said as he plucked a small diamond-shaped piece from the pile.

"That's teak, actually," Chris corrected.

Bell jabbed the plug at him admonishingly. "You get my point." Then he pulled it back and considered. "You should make a cherry one with actual cherries on it."

Chris shook his head, smiling. "Anyone ever tell you that you enjoy your job too much?"

Bell blinked at him and then grinned. "No. Never been true before." Not since he was a ball boy, anyway.

"Well. It suits you." Chris shrugged. He seemed a little shy. "Let me just go get a carpenter square so we can give people a rough idea of dimensions."

"Sure," Bell agreed. He really was enjoying himself, and not only because it meant spending time with Chris. Maybe he *should* e-mail DJ back.

CHAPTER SEVEN

ON SUNDAY, a few hours after Bell called it a day on the dildos, his phone rang.

He looked at it sitting a few feet away from him on the nightstand and then looked back at the DIY show he was watching on Netflix. He wished he could look at the pile of reclaimed wood Chris kept in the shop and come up with that kind of creative repurposing, but seeing Chris do it was pretty cool.

Of course Chris's zillion projects were currently keeping him from snuggling up on the bed with Bell, so it wasn't all antique finishes and artsy decor.

And Bell didn't have a good excuse not to answer the phone. He sighed and picked up without looking at the caller ID. "Hi, Mom."

"Darling, it's so good to hear your voice," she said, as though Bell had been on some remote trek for months.

"I'm not in Siberia, Mom," he protested.

"No, of course not. You're in...." She paused, and maybe it was a little mean, but Bell didn't help her out. If she couldn't even be bothered to remember where he lived.... "Pine Lake," she finished.

Bell rolled his eyes. Pine Lake was his sister's country club. "Close enough," he said dryly. It wasn't like he was dying for her to visit. "How's the family?" He meant, "Who did you call to brag about this time," but his mother raised him better than that. Sort of.

Bell's younger cousin was getting married, apparently to the oldest son of a hedge fund manager. In an unrelated scandal, her older brother had been arrested for driving under the influence. "But you should see Monica," his mother went on, changing tack and tone. "She isn't having an easy pregnancy, poor thing. And with your brother working so much, we've had her over for dinner most nights."

Bell made himself smile. "That's nice of you, Mom."

"Well, it isn't as though she's kept much of it down. But oh, listen to me go on," she tittered. "Tell me what your new life is like, sweetheart. Does Pine Valley have a tennis club?"

"Yes," he said, although it was a guess. A decent-sized university town surely had to have one, not that he intended to find out, unless he had to deliver a pizza there. "But I haven't had a chance to check it out yet."

"Bell, sweetheart, don't let your social life languish. A good club is a great place to meet quality people. You know Crescent Ridge here at home is just full of professional, *creative* types."

Sometimes Bell thought about what it would be like to have homophobic parents, the type who would have kicked him out when he was sixteen and got caught making out with Tyler Bondy behind the bleachers. It would probably suck, but at least he'd have known what to do. As it was, Bell didn't know *what* to do, other than change the subject as fast as possible.

But he wanted to tell her the truth. He liked Chris a lot, and not being able to gush about him to his mom stunk. He knew she loved him, but that love came bundled with a lot of expectations that Bell wouldn't have met even if he were straight.

He wished he could count on her to be excited for him, but he couldn't imagine her taking him dating a—what would she even call Chris? A "working man"?—well. For a few calls, he could probably paint Chris as an entrepreneur. But sooner or later—

No, his first instinct was right. Better to avoid the subject. Especially since he had a diversionary tactic handy. "I'm worrying about work right now," he said. "I got an e-mail from that recruiter you sent my way. He wants to have lunch."

His mom snapped up the bait and gushed about this DJ person. "Well, he comes highly recommended. Elaine Zimmerman—you know Elaine, we always work together on the league charity auction— DJ is a friend of her nephew's, and he left a very lucrative position at one of those big-four firms to strike out on his own. He found the corporate world too stuffy."

Bell nodded along. That didn't sound so bad, but then his mom continued and Bell got the catch, which he really should have seen coming.

"Elaine tells me that in addition to being quite successful, DJ is a confirmed bachelor. I think the two of you might have a lot in common."

"Mom," he protested. "I'm not really looking for a relationship right now." Technically not a lie, since he was in one, but he still felt guilty.

"I just want you to think about your future. You won't be young forever, you know. You don't want to end up like your uncle."

Privately Bell thought there were worse fates than dying a rich philanthropic pervert, but his mother wouldn't agree. "I'll be fine, Mom. I've only been here a little while. I have lots of time to make friends." He'd made a few already, though if he told her about Jenny, he'd probably let slip that he worked as a pizza delivery boy, so he decided to keep his mouth shut.

Lady Frances chose that moment to materialize from under the bed. She poked the screen with her nose for a few moments and then opted to massage Bell's lap into a more comfortable shape. "Meanwhile I sort of have a cat. It's not like I'm lonely."

"A cat!" his mother exclaimed. "I always wanted a cat, you know."

"Really?" For once she sounded completely genuine, and about something Bell never would have guessed.

"My mother had a Ragdoll when I was growing up. Sweet old thing. But your father's allergic, so of course we can't have one."

Bell tried to imagine his mother as a teenager, with her always immaculate, fashionable clothing coated in a layer of shed fur and a big, lazy cat in her arms. He utterly failed and shook his head. "This one's named Lady Frances, and I sort of inherited her with the apartment. I'm in charge of feeding her, but she comes and goes as she pleases."

His mother laughed. "Well, of course. She's a cat."

"Not a bad life," Bell said, scratching Lady Frances under her chin. She purred and then flopped bonelessly across his lap and rubbed her head on his thigh.

"Oh, you would think so, wouldn't you," his mother said, but she sounded fond, none of the usual reproach in her tone. "I've got to go, darling. There's a league charity board meeting tonight. Spoil your cat for me."

Bell promised and hung up the phone.

Lady Frances stared at him from his lap, her eyes narrowed to slits.

With a sigh Bell restarted Netflix, reaching out to hit the button with his toe so he wouldn't have to disturb the cat. Then he took Lady Frances's hint and rubbed behind her ears. "Well, you're not the snuggle partner I'd have picked first," he admitted. Oh God, he was talking to a cat. "But you're pretty cute anyway."

WHEN THE episode of *Make It Again, Sam* finished, Bell watched the bloopers that ran behind the credits and then looked at his watch. He thought that he and Chris had agreed to meet up for dinner, but Chris hadn't called yet. Bell didn't want to interfere with Chris's bathroom tiling project—he'd seen enough renovation shows to know that once the adhesive went on the subfloor, you couldn't exactly take a break for make-outs. But he was also getting a little cross-eyed after staring at dildos and taking their portraits all day.

He got off the bed and stretched. Then he went downstairs for a cup of coffee. The workshop was quiet, with a few lingering rays of late-afternoon sunlight coming through the windows. He decided to give Chris another hour. Maybe this was a good time to catch up on his e-mail, or maybe even to call that friend of Elaine's.

Oh, and it was definitely a good time to feed the cat, who was staring at him judgmentally from the countertop when he trotted back upstairs. "You could've just said something," Bell pointed out as he opened the cupboard underneath Lady Frances's seat and retrieved the cat food. He fished a clean bowl from the dishwasher, filled it, and dug his cell phone out of his pocket.

He had DJ saved in his contacts, but he hesitated to press Send. If he was going to take that step, he was going to do it right. He at least wanted a copy of his résumé in front of him so he could reference it if he blanked on what to say.

As it turned out, though, he took the precaution for nothing. "Hi, you've reached DJ at Golden Globe Recruiting. I'm out of the office until Monday morning, but if you leave your name and number, I'll get back to you as soon as possible. If this is regarding a position that needs filling immediately, please hang up and call our office directly. Someone will be happy to take your call."

Bell left a brief message with his phone number and then flopped back on the bed and pulled his laptop closer to look up a restaurant someone had recommended to him when he delivered their pizza.

Ten minutes later he headed out the door—or he meant to, but Joseph was sitting at the front desk, tapping a pencil absently on a textbook and scrolling through something on the computer.

"Working late?" Bell asked and leaned over the edge of the desk.

Joseph jumped a foot off the chair. "Jesus. Warn a guy."

Apparently he'd been in the zone. "Sorry. What're you still doing here, though?" The shop had closed hours before.

"Ugh." Joseph rubbed his eyes. "Picking my courses for next semester. I was trying to work out a schedule that'd let me be here more often. I guess it's taking longer than I thought."

"All right. Well, I'll leave you to it, then. Good luck."

The restaurant he looked up earlier had a website, but it only had their phone number and a few customer reviews. Bell wanted to see the menu, get a sense of the food they offered, and figure out the prices before he committed to an order, sight unseen. Fortunately the place was exactly between Bell's apartment and Chris's house. It was a hole-in-the-wall with only four tables, but there were five people ahead of him in the take-out line. The menu promised both Thai and Malaysian dishes, and every plate Bell saw looked fantastic and smelled even better, so he ordered a few different things and waited until the take-out server handed him two bags and a menu that was far more comprehensive than the website.

He looked at his phone: 8:07 p.m. Between feeding the cat, leaving the message for DJ, and waiting for his food, he'd killed more than an hour. But no missed calls and still no word from Chris. And honestly Bell was starting to feel a little faint. He needed to eat.

Reasoning that Chris probably needed to eat too, he set the take-out bag on the Malibu's passenger seat and drove to Chris's.

He didn't experience any doubts until he pulled into the driveway.

What if Chris didn't want to see him? What if he hadn't called because he changed his mind and decided he didn't want to date Bell, after all? What if he was just moody and wanted to be alone for a night? Bell certainly had days like that.

Well, if that was what Chris wanted, he would have to say so sooner or later, because Bell was about to die of starvation, and he planned to eat, unless Chris told him to get lost. He picked up the take-out bags and got out of the car. Then he climbed the kitchen steps, stopped, and put the bags down. Maybe Chris was sick or asleep or—

The front door opened.

"Bell! I thought I heard your car. I'm so sorry. I lost track of time and didn't even realize how late it had gotten." Chris's hair was rumpled, there was paint on his cheek, and his knees were spattered with grout.

"It's a good thing I brought dinner, then." Bell leaned down to pick up the bags and handed them to Chris. "Hope you like Thai. I stopped by that little place by the laundromat."

"How long did you have to wait in line?" Chris stepped back, brushing at his hair without much luck. "Thai House is always backed up this time of day."

"Not long," Bell said. "But I hope you're hungry, because I might have ordered enough to get us through the week." He went into the kitchen, put the bags on the counter, and opened the cupboards to find plates and bowls.

"Not those," Chris said and opened another cupboard. "Use the good china—well, the good pottery, anyway."

"Don't tell me you're also a potter," Bell said. "A guy could get an inferiority complex."

Chris blushed, or at least Bell thought he saw pink underneath the paint. "Just fairly good at bartering," he said. "Look, let me go shower and then we can eat?"

Great, now Bell had to contend with his rumbling stomach *and* the knowledge that Chris was getting wet and naked just a few rooms over. On the other hand, at least Chris hadn't blown Bell off on purpose. And the grubby look worked for him. "Shower fast," he said. "I'm about to expire on your floor."

Chris made an apologetic noise of distress, leaned in for a kiss, and then appeared to think better of it. He pulled back and looked down at his clothes and hands. "Table that for later," he said ruefully. "I don't want to get you dirty."

Now that was a shame. But Bell smiled and waved him off. "Go. I'll set the table."

Chris went.

To his credit, he didn't keep Bell waiting much longer. Bell only had to stave off the other hunger—the one fueled by his imagination and the sound of running water—for long enough to find the appropriate plates, bowls, cutlery, and napkins. By the time he took the food out of the bag, Chris reappeared, wearing nice jeans and a Henley shirt that clung to his body. It looked like maybe he hadn't dried off very thoroughly.

"Go ahead. You can go wash up and I'll finish out here," Chris said.

"Okay." Bell went to the bathroom to wash his hands, the better not to be underfoot, and took the opportunity to try to pat his hair into slightly better shape. When he got back to the table, Chris was just lighting the second of a pair of candles and a bottle of wine was uncorked on the table.

"I just brought over a few cartons of takeout," Bell said.

"I just completely lost track of time and kept my date waiting all night while I tiled a bathroom." Chris poured a glass of wine and set the bottle down. Then he pulled Bell in by the belt and kissed him, soft but not exactly chaste. Bell was just settling in to enjoy the press of Chris's mouth when Chris backed away again. "I'm hoping I can romance my way to forgiveness."

As if Bell could stay mad. "Well, normally you'd be further ahead with the kissing than the candles, but my stomach is starting to eat itself."

A low, growly rumble filled the room.

Bell blinked. "Was that your stomach?"

"I might have also skipped lunch?"

"Okay, food now, kissing later." Bell pulled out a chair, coaxed Chris to sit, and took the spot next to him. They made quick inroads into the food, which was delicious enough to fully explain the line at the restaurant.

"This is really great," Bell said when his stomach realized he was going to continue feeding it and stopped complaining so loudly. "I'm finding nice surprises in Pineville every day."

"We suck you in with simple small-town charm, then seduce you with…." Chris trailed off and then looked thoughtful. "Better-than-expected Asian food, I suppose. We're not really teeming with hidden secrets."

"Fine artisan dildos," Bell suggested.

Chris grinned and nudged his foot under the table. "I don't know. Usually people do the seducing before the dildos come into play."

Then he seemed to realize what he'd said, and he groaned.

"I must just be special, since I got the dildos upfront and all," Bell said, completely failing to keep a straight face.

"That offer is definitely only for VIPs."

Bell smiled at his dinner plate. "So. Tiling the bathroom. Really? Don't you get enough work in during work hours?"

"I told you, I don't like to sit still." Chris shrugged. "Maybe I need to get some more relaxing hobbies, though."

"I'm sure we can think of one or two," Bell said, suddenly impatient to have their plates empty. He took another sip of wine. "You're not at a stage where you have to go directly back to work right after dinner, are you?"

Chris grinned back at him. Apparently he was running hot rather than cold. "I can afford to take a little time off. Did you have something in mind?"

Bell considered the wooden dining chairs. They were handmade and sturdy, but probably not enough for what he was thinking. The sofa, though. That would be perfect. "Maybe we can have dessert in the other room."

From the expression on Chris's face, he'd seen the bottom of the bag and knew Bell hadn't really brought dessert. "You weren't kidding about your appetite."

"It's voracious," Bell agreed. He had too much pride to go for the obvious "I'll eat you up" line, but it was close. "Are you finished? Because I'm in the mood for something sweet, and I feel like it would be rude to start without you."

Chris snuffed a laugh. "I think I've had enough."

"Thank God." Bell wanted to get his hands all over that damp cotton—maybe more than his hands, if he were lucky. He refilled their wineglasses and stood up. "Come on and make me comfortable."

The couch was the opposite of the one Bell owned in his last apartment. That one was expensive, sleek, and far better to look at than to relax—much less do anything else—on. Chris's sofa was older, had definitely seen some wear, and was just soft enough to encourage a bit of a sprawl.

"See, this is much nicer." He set down his glass and patted the spot next to him.

Chris obediently settled down beside him, but when Bell reached out to pull him closer, Chris tugged him right onto his lap.

Definitely hot. Bell would have to be careful not to push until he ran cold again.

"And even better." He shifted until he was straddling Chris's thighs, then decided he might as well go for it and threaded his fingers through Chris's hair too. It slid smoothly through his fingers, soft and thick, still damp from Chris's shower and warm with his body heat.

Chris settled his hands on Bell's hips, thumbs teasing over his pelvic bones. "You think so?"

"Mmm-hmm," Bell said, shifting his weight. Chris's eyes darkened. "It's almost perfect."

"Really. And how can we make it—"

Bell kissed him.

Chris responded instantly, opening his mouth against Bell's. Bell loved the way Chris kissed him, deep and languid, as though he'd be happy to do it for hours. He tilted his head back so Chris could nuzzle his throat. Bell found himself hoping for at least a little trace of beard burn. Chris nipped at a particularly sensitive spot and made Bell writhe in his lap. Bell was already getting hard, and he hoped Chris wouldn't be too tired to enjoy that, at least a little, even if enjoy it was all he did.

Chris paused in scraping his teeth over Bell's lower lip. He bit him and made a hot, low noise into Bell's mouth. So no. He wasn't that tired.

Good.

Before Bell could find a rhythm of his own, Chris moved his hands down and tucked his fingers into Bell's back pockets. For a second Bell thought Chris intended to keep Bell still while feeling him up, which he understood. Chris kept saying he wanted to take it slow.

But then Chris pulled him forward, tilting Bell's hips as he did. Bell's brain fizzled a little, because he was well past *getting* hard and so was Chris, and he couldn't remember the last time touching someone had felt so good.

He must have muttered something to that effect, because Chris murmured a "yeah" between kisses. Bell rocked his hips, making Chris moan into his mouth. They were getting somewhere.

Bell ran his hands over Chris's shoulders and teased at the placket of the Henley with his thumbs. It had been a long time since he needed this kind of coordination and concentration. Chris's hands were strong and warm against his ass, his mouth drove Bell to distraction, and Bell ached to touch him everywhere. He slid his hands farther, until he could feel the muscled strength of Chris's chest, and spread his hands so his fingers brushed against Chris's nipples.

Chris inhaled sharply—he liked that as much as Bell did—and dug his fingers in a little harder to control the roll of Bell's hips.

Bell stopped thinking and let it happen.

At some point they lost a fight with gravity and common sense and listed to one side, but Chris only kicked his feet up on the couch and took Bell's weight on his chest as well as his lap. If Chris didn't want to stop, Bell wasn't going to. He pushed up on his arms so he could slot his leg between Chris's without squashing anything important, and then Chris pulled him back in.

So much body contact, after he'd been starving for it for so long, threatened to overwhelm him. From the way Chris moved his hands, Bell thought he might feel the same. He caressed from Bell's ass to his back to his shoulders to his nape, until he cradled Bell's head and his thumbs brushed the sensitive skin behind Bell's ears.

They kissed until Bell's chin hurt from beard burn and his dick protested too much. Then, as if by mutual agreement, they backed off. Chris tilted his head into the cushions as Bell breathed into his neck. "I feel like I'm seventeen again," Chris said ruefully, stroking Bell's back.

Bell smiled against his shoulder. "I don't. I definitely would've come in my pants if I did this when I was seventeen."

Chris's groan vibrated through Bell's chest and almost tickled. "Don't tease."

"You're the one who pulled me onto your lap."

"Sorry." Chris brushed his fingers through Bell's hair. It felt nice. Maybe he should grow it out so Chris had more to play with. He'd wanted to wear it long when he was younger, but his mother insisted it looked unprofessional. "I'm not trying to be a tease. I know it's—"

"It's fine," Bell finished for him, raising a finger to Chris's lips. "This is fun, actually. Inconvenient side effects aside." He'd missed out on this in high school, and in college he and his boyfriend skipped over the hours-long-make-outs stage.

Chris tilted his head down to meet Bell's gaze. The odd angle gave him an unattractive double chin. "Yeah?"

Bell liked him so much. He didn't need to have sex with him to enjoy the time they spent together. And he'd had more delicious body contact with Chris in the past week than he'd had with anyone in longer than he could remember. He hadn't even known how skin-hungry he was. "Yeah." He could tell his own expression probably looked kind of stupid, but he didn't care.

He wasn't even really disappointed when Chris broke the sweet moment with a yawn that he muffled in the back of the couch.

Bell could take a hint, even an involuntary one. "I should probably go." On a whim, he leaned up and pressed a kiss to Chris's chin. "It's not like I won't see you when I head out for work tomorrow."

With some difficulty, he managed to avoid maiming Chris when he sat up.

"You're too good for me," Chris told him. He took his hands and pulled him into one more chaste kiss.

"You just haven't witnessed my bad habits yet." Bell wondered about the etiquette and then adjusted himself. Chris had had Bell's erection pressed into his hip for the past who knew how long; it wasn't like he didn't know it was there. "Give it a few more weeks. I'm sure you'll be singing a different tune."

The voiced assumption that they'd still be together in a few weeks earned him a fond-eyed look. "We'll see."

Chris walked him to his car, even though it was parked in Chris's driveway. Bell couldn't remember anyone else having done that. It was endearing.

Bell was still endeared when Chris pushed him gently against the side of the Malibu and kissed him again, soft and thorough, until Bell pulled him closer, never mind that he'd *just* convinced his dick it wasn't going to get any action tonight. At least not from Chris. The air and the side of the car were cold, but Chris kept him warm until he pulled away with a kiss to Bell's cheek. "See you tomorrow."

Bell was probably wearing that dumb expression again. "Good night."

He let the car's engine run for a few moments and then backed down the driveway. His knees were still shaky.

CHAPTER EIGHT

ONE WEDNESDAY a few weeks later, Bell breezed into the shop just past noon, balancing a pizza box on his shoulder. He'd been delivering Chris's Wednesday noon pizza for over a month now. Today he was going to get answers.

"Hey, Joseph," he said cheerfully over the sound of a saw singing in the workshop. He put the pizza on the counter. "I'm assuming the boss man is hard at work."

Joseph looked up from what he was doing—from the looks of things, mailing overdue invoices. Praise God. Chris could be taught. Or at least taught to delegate. "How'd you guess?" he asked wryly.

Bell grinned. "I'm gonna go bug him, okay?"

"I'm sure he'll be very annoyed." Joseph was already nose deep in invoices again.

Bell left the food on the counter to avoid sawdust contamination and stuck his head into the workshop. "Order's up," he said when Chris noticed him and stopped the saw.

Chris pulled his headphones off and moved closer. "What?"

Never mind. "How come you order pizza delivered when you work right across the street?"

"I'm bad at remembering to take lunch breaks."

"So what, you wait until you're too hungry to think and call for delivery?"

Chris nodded toward the saw. "Nah. I set it up ahead of time. Trust me, that is not something you want to mess with when you're dizzy or cranky from hunger."

Bell looked at the sharp teeth of the saw and back at Chris's hands. "Definitely not."

"Besides, it's not like I eat out a lot. It's a treat, it's cheap, and Wednesday lunch isn't the busiest time, so I never have to wait long."

"If we don't come in thirty minutes, it's free," Bell quipped and then realized what he'd said.

Chris cleared his throat and grinned. The tips of his ears were red.

"Shut up," Bell said before he could make it worse. He hoped poor Joseph hadn't overheard.

"What's it cost if it's under thirty minutes?" Chris asked. He grabbed Bell by the waist and tugged him close.

Sighing, Bell checked the receipt in his hand. "Twelve fifty."

"A bargain at twice the price," Chris teased and kissed him.

Never in a million years, Bell thought ruefully, was it going to take longer than thirty minutes—unless Chris decided to tease him to death. "I have to go," he said after a minute, pulling away and rubbing at his chin. He would have to see about some kind of cream for stubble rash. "I just wanted to, well"—he gestured at Chris—"ask about your weird pizza-ordering habit."

"Did I mention the new delivery boy is cute?" Chris said innocently.

"Oh, well, now that I know you're the kind of guy with shady motives," Bell teased.

"Now what?"

"Now I know I have to meet up with you under the cover of darkness, lest my reputation suffer."

"Get out of here, you." Chris leaned in to peck him on the cheek. "Can't have you consorting with unsavory types on the clock."

With a smile on his face and a spring to his step, Bell left Chris to his lunch. His good mood was so apparent that Jenny shook her head when he came back in for the next pickup. "You are enjoying this day way too much."

"I'm in a good mood."

"Great. Take your good mood and these fifteen ultrameat specials up to Phi House."

"You got it." Bell wasn't even bothered by the prospect of a trip up to the top of Frat Hill with a sausage-and-anchovy-scented armload for a dollar tip with a side offer of a joint and a party invitation.

It just proved that his day was great when not only was his tip decent—and in paper money, even—but when he got back to the car, he had a voice mail.

"Hi, Bellamy. This is DJ from Golden Globe Recruiting. Sorry for not calling back sooner, but I had to reschedule my trip to Pineville because I needed to be on the West Coast for business. I'm in town tomorrow and Friday, though, and I'd love to get together to discuss some opportunities."

Perfect. Bell put his Bluetooth headset in as he pulled around the circular drive. He called DJ back to make a lunch date for Friday.

HIS LAST delivery of the night had him schlepping calzones to a dance studio halfway between the university and one of the grade schools. A woman who couldn't have been taller than five feet or heavier than ninety pounds answered and let him in. All the bills were separate, so payment would take a while. "You must be the new guy," she said as she easily took half of the dinners and balanced them with one hand. "Come on in. Sorry. We're just going over our plan for the next quarter, and we're all too hungry to think."

"You know, you're not the first people I've met with that problem today." Bell set his stack of boxes on the table and looked at the receipts. His customers had the lights dimmed to watch a PowerPoint presentation—the current slide read Marketing at the top but was otherwise blank—so he had to squint a little in the darkness.

"Oh, let me get the light," the woman said. "I'm Kathy, by the way."

"Bell, but around here I also go by New Guy." Even though it'd been more than a month. It seemed that aside from the college students, Pineville didn't get fresh blood too often. He blinked when the lights came on and then couldn't help but nod at the projector screen. "Stuck for ideas?"

"We're pretty much word of mouth," Kathy said, "but I think we have to start doing something besides just using our personal e-mails." She began to distribute the boxes around the table.

"No website?"

One of the women wrinkled her nose. "None of us have kids old enough to make something that looks professional, and our budget probably doesn't match what an actual marketing person would suggest."

Bell tried not to wince. "What about up at the college? I bet they have bulletin boards you could advertise on, like if you wanted to do a group class to teach a salsa or something." The sorority girls would definitely be into it. They always had the furniture pushed against the walls in the living room to make a bigger dance space. "You could even have one of your students go in before one of the freshman classes, the crowded ones everyone has to take."

Kathy exchanged glances with the lone man at the table, who looked to be just a bit older than Bell. Then she looked back at him. "Are you taking marketing in school?"

"No," Bell said. "I mean, I did major in marketing, but that was a few years back, before I went to work as a marketing consultant in an enormous global firm."

"But you're a pizza delivery guy," Kathy said. There was a tiny wrinkle between her eyebrows. "How does that work?"

Bell stifled the impulse to explain how delivery service generally worked, and gave her his most dazzling smile instead. "I also do some small-business consulting, but I like not spending eighteen hours a day in a cubicle."

The guy laughed in obvious surprise. "Yeah, I definitely get that. I think we all do, actually."

"I miss when I didn't have to pretend I like bookkeeping," one of the women agreed. "Needs must with a small business. You know."

"I'm starting to, yeah." Bell flipped over one of the receipts and scrawled his cell phone number. "I haven't had any business cards made up yet, but if you want to give me a call, I can come in for a consult. No obligation, free of charge, yadda yadda."

Bell left the dance studio with a nice tip and a smile on his face at the idea of getting to use his craft in a much less pressured environment. He slid into his car and shot Chris a text—*Hey, you still up?*—but by the time he pulled into his parking space behind the pizza shop, he didn't have a reply. *Guess not,* he sent and told himself he wasn't disappointed. It would have been nice to share the day's triumphs with Chris, but it was late. Of course Chris had gone to bed.

Bell frowned down at his phone and wondered if leaving the text thread there made him sound needy and passive-aggressive. He didn't want Chris to wake up and look at his phone first thing and think Bell was annoyed. *Sweet dreams xox,* he added and then shoved his phone in his pocket. There. Who could mind waking up to that?

He grabbed his jacket from the passenger seat, locked the car, and went into the restaurant to clock out, forcing a smile at Jenny behind the bar. He *wasn't* disappointed. He just wanted to wish Chris good night. That was all, he told himself.

Jenny evidently wasn't fooled. "What happened to your good mood?" she asked gently as she set aside a stack of dirty plates.

Bell knew she meant well, but he didn't know if he wanted to get into it. It seemed rude to talk to her about Chris when she'd known him longer. "Nothing," he lied.

Jenny raised her eyebrows. "Uh-huh. Me too."

For the first time since he'd come in, Bell noticed that her makeup seemed too fresh, as though she'd had to reapply it.

He picked up the stack of plates, put them in the plastic bin, and walked toward to the kitchen. "Tell you what," he said. "Let's finish closing out, and then I have some Netflix and beer with our names on them."

"You don't have to," Jenny said, though he could hear the hope in her voice. "You're off shift. No more deliveries."

"True, but if I don't clock out, Antonio will probably still pay me, and it's not like I have anywhere better to be."

"That's the problem, huh?" she said knowingly as they started loading the dishwasher.

Bell blew out a long breath and wiped a smear of marinara sauce off a plate. "All right. I'm kind of bummed out because Chris wasn't around to share my excitement about some good news. That's sort of the point of having a boyfriend, you know? I mean, I get that he works zillion-hour days, so he's probably in bed—alone, *sleeping*. But I don't know. Sometimes I feel like he's avoiding me, which is dumb."

Jenny wrinkled her nose. "Maybe he needs space? He's a brooder."

"Maybe." That seemed close enough to the truth for Bell to feel a bit better, as though something inside him had unwound a bit. He retrieved another bin of dirty dishes and started to load them up. During the busy hours, Antonio had kitchen staff to do that, but they went home after the dinner rush. "Okay, your turn."

Jenny jammed the last dish into the tray, closed the dishwasher, and started the cycle. "A friend of mine got accepted to medical school."

"Okay," Bell repeated. Jenny had never mentioned anything about wanting to be a doctor, had she?

"In Switzerland," she continued on a long breath.

Ah. Well, that made more sense. "You're going to miss her?" Bell guessed.

Jenny tried a smile. It wobbled long before it had a chance of meeting her eyes.

"Oh," Bell said. Oh, that sucked. He probably didn't have enough beer for this. "Okay, let's finish up here, because we need to get ice cream." He'd never nursed a friend through a broken heart before, but Netflix had led him to believe this was the correct course of action.

Netflix must have been right, because Jenny managed a smile. "That sounds nice."

LADY FRANCES cleared out as soon as she finished eating, as though she sensed some complicated human thing was happening and decided it was beneath her. Bell wanted to shower off the pizza smell, but instead he put the ice cream on the counter and dug out a couple of spoons.

Jenny spilled her guts, they ate ice cream, and Bell listened and wondered if he were supposed to say anything—until the carton was empty and Jenny looked at it, spoon raised, as though she didn't understand where its contents had gone.

Then she laughed a bit and wiped the makeup smears from under her eyes. "God. I can't believe we ate that much. You must think I'm a pig."

"I am actually impressed," Bell corrected. Then he paused and patted his own stomach. "And possibly a little bloated."

"God. Same."

They weathered the storm of ice cream cramps leaning against the headboard of Bell's bed, watching *Notting Hill* on Netflix. By the time it was over, Bell was yawning and Jenny had actually fallen asleep. He gently shook her awake and offered her a ride home, but she declined.

"I'm just parked beside the Rabbit," she assured him. "And it's a short drive. I'll be fine."

Lady Frances slinked back in when Jenny had gone, and stared at Bell judgmentally from the rolltop desk until Bell showered and brushed his teeth.

When he finally climbed into bed, he found himself looking forward to Friday's lunch. Maybe this DJ guy would have something a little steadier than gigs he could get from writing on the back of a receipt. It would be good to have the money and a little more security, especially if he could work from home most of the time. On the other hand, the referral came from someone with a vested interest in Bell

106

going back to the corporate world—and that wasn't going to happen. At least not now and maybe not for a long time, if things worked out the way Bell wanted them to.

He sighed and flipped his pillow over to the cool side. Lady Frances patted him on the cheek, claws only slightly extended, then turned around and curled against Bell's thigh. Bell drifted off to sleep with only a passing thought about whether Chris had gotten his texts.

BELL AND DJ had arranged to meet for lunch at the diner near the university, so Bell slung his laptop into his messenger bag and slipped out the door of the shop while Chris was chatting with Denise, the mail carrier, about a custom kitchen table. He waved, and Chris waved back, and then Bell was out the door.

He got to the diner early to set up at a quiet table—he knew from driving by that it could get crowded around lunch—and passed a handful of minutes drafting ideas he could bring to Kathy at their meeting.

The bells on the door jingled, and Bell glanced up. A man in skinny jeans and a white shirt stood in the doorway. He changed his aviator sunglasses for an indoor pair with rectangular lenses and then looked around the diner until he spotted Bell.

Bell shut down his laptop and put it back in his bag.

"Excuse me. Bell?"

"Yes," Bell said. He stood and offered his hand. "DJ?"

"That's me," DJ said as he slid into the booth. "Your mom sent me a picture so I could find you, but you don't exactly look Pineville, so I think I could have managed on my own."

"That's only a little creepy," Bell said without thinking. Apparently he'd forgotten how to play nice in the corporate world after just a few weeks' freedom. Oh well.

DJ didn't seem offended. He just shot him a slightly greasy smile and reached for one of the menus tucked against the side of the booth. "When you travel as much as I do, you notice things that seem out of place."

Bell didn't know what to say to that, so he left it alone and changed the subject. "Do you come through this way often?"

DJ wiggled his hand from side to side. "Now and again. I used to live here, for a bit, but the small-town life wasn't for me."

That, Bell had no trouble believing. "It agrees with me so far." Then he second-guessed himself and added, "But who knows what the future holds, right?" He didn't want to limit his options right off the bat, even if that meant stretching the truth.

"Exactly." DJ frowned at the menu, then put it aside and gave Bell a big smile. "So, Elaine told me you're stuck in Pineville and looking for options."

"I'm not stuck," Bell said. "Haven't been here long enough for that. Like I said, it's working out so far."

"How would you feel about coming in on the ground floor of a new boutique firm? I promise no more than 60 percent travel. Corporate credit card, they would lease a car for you, all the stuff that only the top tier gets in the big firms."

Bell raised a shoulder and let it drop. "Sounds a notch above standard, yeah. What's their segment and client list look like?"

"It's a little bit of everything right now," DJ said. "You know start-ups, but they're hoping to concentrate on privately held consumer products. I understand you've done some marketing campaigns for that sector."

Yeah, but I was the rookie. "I've been on a few teams," he said. Their server dropped off a couple of glasses and filled them with ice water, and Bell made himself slow his breathing and take a sip to calm down. This didn't have to mean anything. DJ could call him all he liked. Bell didn't have to say yes. He didn't even have to pick up the phone.

But did he really want to deliver pizza his whole life?

That internal voice sounded a little too much like his mother for comfort.

"Have you had a chance to look at the menu?" the server asked.

DJ didn't look up. "I'll have a gingerbread latte, skim milk, hold the whip, and the house burger, medium, extra pickles, pickles on the side, mayo instead of ketchup for the fries."

He had definitely been here before, then. "Sweet tea, please. Um, what's the soup of the day?" Bell could use something to warm him from the inside. Though the prospect of spilling it down his chin in front of DJ soon made him reconsider.

"Split pea," the server said. "It's okay."

Bell smiled at her. "Short stack of chocolate-chip pancakes and a side of bacon instead, then."

"Gotcha," she said and smiled back at him, though she walked away without acknowledging DJ.

"This place," DJ said, still looking at his phone. "What's a guy like you even doing here?"

"Same thing anyone does, I guess. Working, trying new things, seeing the world." Bell waited until DJ finished whatever he was doing on his phone and looked up. Then he steeled himself to make some small talk until their food arrived. But after a few minutes of chitchat, the suspense and his curiosity got the better of him. "I have to say I'm not really sure why you e-mailed me, other than that Elaine passed my number along to you. I wasn't planning on going back to corporate for a while."

"She says good things about you." DJ shrugged and winked at Bell. "She also said you were kind of cute. Sue me. I was intrigued."

Bell didn't have to answer right away because the server arrived with their food. He leaned back so she could put down his pancakes and DJ's burger. She left and then returned with a side plate full of pickles. Bell squashed his smile as DJ reached for the pickles before the plate was even on the table.

"These pickles are the only thing I miss about Pineville," DJ said as he reached for more.

"Yeah, you said you lived here."

"We all make mistakes." DJ popped a pickle into his mouth, wiped his fingers on a napkin, and reached for his latte. "Waste of a few months. But hey, maybe you'll be better suited." His expression clearly said he didn't think so. "Anyway, let's eat, and then I bet you brought a portfolio to show off?"

Bell's stomach twisted, but he managed to choke down his pancakes without reaching across the table to throttle DJ. At least, since DJ was a recruiter and not actually an in-house HR staffer, this job likely wouldn't involve working closely with him. He didn't want to offend the guy, but he also didn't want to give the impression he was looking forward to seeing him again, especially in anything more than a professional capacity.

When the server cleared their plates, DJ made grabby hands for Bell's laptop. "Okay, show me the goods."

Bell licked a stray drop of syrup from his thumb, then had to hide his wince when DJ leered at him. He opened his computer. "I've got some older mock-ups from the bigger projects I worked on as part of a group, but those aren't entirely my work. This one is, though." He opened the presentation he'd started for the dance studio. "It's a small business looking to increase its web presence and expand its target audience to include students at the college, but they're not sure how to go about it."

"Most people aren't," DJ said, pulling the computer toward himself, tilted so Bell could no longer see the screen. "You're thinking website, Twitter, word of mouth?"

"Maybe Instagram or Facebook too, if they're interested, but what they really need is an event to get the students interested in the first place. I've got a couple ideas—offer a free class or a cheap group lesson, or throw some kind of dance mixer that's part party, part opportunity to learn from good young dancers." And hit on them and be hit on *by* them, of course, but Bell left that part unsaid.

"Mmm," DJ said absently. He paged through the presentation so fast there was no way he could be paying much attention. "Have to be careful not to oversaturate with social media, though."

Bell bristled. He knew that. He wasn't a freshman. "Of course. Different types of content for different platforms. Just have to figure out what type of content they're going to create first. I wanted to cover all the bases for the presentation."

"Of course," DJ echoed, sounding bored. He pushed the laptop away.

"It sounds like your clients are looking for something different," Bell said as he closed his laptop. "Can you describe a typical project?"

"A lot bigger than a dance studio," DJ said. "No offense, but small towns have small minds and small budgets."

"They still need marketing help, though."

DJ slumped against the back of the booth and took a deep drink of his latte. When he put the cup down, there was a distinct foam mustache on his upper lip. "That's what college interns are for, Bell. You have to think bigger. Don't you want to fly first class or drive a Porsche or splash out on trips for your buddies to Vegas or the beach? Big deals make that happen faster."

The bells on the door jangled again, but Bell ignored them in favor of leaning across the table. "Listen," he said, trying not to imagine the look Jenny would give him if he offered to take her to Vegas, "I get where you're going with this, but I tried that already and hated it. I'm not the kind of guy who's out every night with his squad. I'd rather stay at home and cook dinner"—okay, have Chris make him dinner—"maybe learn how to do stuff around the house, come home at a reasonable hour."

"You should date my ex," DJ said.

"Not on the market," Bell said.

"But your mom—"

"Doesn't know squat," Bell said, and motioned to the server for the check. "Your client's plans sound awesome, DJ, and if they've got some contract work available, I'd love to stay on their call list. I'm not ready to go back to a firm at this point, though."

DJ shook his head. "You're turning down a golden opportunity here, Bell."

"Yeah, well, I'd rather live in a wood barn than a gilded cage." Bell paid for both their lunches, just to prove he didn't give a fuck about money, and left a nice tip too. "The pancakes were great," he told the server as he stood. "Pass my compliments to the chef."

DJ craned his neck up at him and narrowed his eyes, assessing. "You have gumption, I'll give you that."

Bell managed a crooked smile he didn't quite feel. "Well, when it's the only thing you've got, you have to play to your strengths. I'm serious about that contract work, though. You know how to reach me."

By focusing very hard on the door, he managed to make it outside and partway through the alley to the parking lot before his heart rate climbed too high and he had to lean against the brick wall of the building and concentrate on breathing. He felt like he was going to puke, or pass out, or die.

A few minutes passed, the bands around his chest loosened, and the gray dots in his vision disappeared. Even when he could stand again, Bell felt wrung-out, almost hungover. But at least he knew one thing for sure: no matter what happened, he couldn't go back to a corporate office.

It would kill him.

CHAPTER NINE

BELL SPENT the rest of the afternoon being as un-consultant-like as possible while actually doing consulting work. He changed into his oldest, softest pair of jeans, a pair of wool socks in bright neon stripes, and a T-shirt with a defunct sports team's logo. He pulled his laptop onto the bed to work on some ideas for Kathy as well as some text for Chris's dildo shop, with Lady Frances as his only colleague. She leaned against his thigh with her paw in the air so she could lick at the base of her tail.

"And yet you're still a lot better mannered than my lunch companion."

Lady Frances didn't look up. The sentiment stood, though.

When his stomach started making noises and demanded those pancakes be replaced with dinner, he saved his work and checked the time. He could text Chris, sure. But Bell could hear him sanding something, so he slid on a pair of shoes and went downstairs.

Chris had taken off his overshirt and wore a T-shirt that clung to his biceps, shoulders, and chest, as he sanded an armoire that would stand at least eight feet tall. At the moment, though, it sat on its side on a pair of sawhorses, laid out for Chris to work his magic.

Wow. Bell had been doing okay on the no-sex front until now. Or at least he'd been doing okay breaking in Chris's merchandise instead of Chris himself.

He waved at Chris to get his attention without interrupting, and then he took a seat in the old chair pushed to the side. Chris nodded at him but kept on working for a few minutes. Bell tried to make himself believe he wasn't disappointed. When Chris apparently got to a satisfactory stopping place, he switched off the sander and looked

113

at where Bell was sprawled with his feet propped on what he'd come to think of as his crate.

"You look quite at home," Chris said. He was smiling, but he was still, frustratingly, standing on the far side of the armoire.

"I bet I would look a lot better if some sawdust happened to get transferred to my person," he said, raising his eyebrows hopefully.

That got him a cute snort. Chris shook his head, came over, and then leaned down and ruffled his hair right over Bell's chest.

"Not what I had in mind," Bell huffed.

Chris looked up at him with a fond expression, but something in it seemed reserved. Still, Bell got his kiss and leaned back farther in his chair to entice Chris to press closer. He smelled like sawdust and honest sweat. Bell's mother would not approve, but nobody had asked her. "Mmm," Bell said happily when Chris pulled away. "Hi. Get lots done today?"

Chris gestured expansively to the armoire. "Pardon the pun, but I have my work cut out for me."

Bell rolled his eyes but grinned anyway, so Chris continued. "It's actually been a lot of fun to do. It's for a lady over in Mount Kelley. She's redone one of the old hunting lodges up there into something that could be in *Architectural Digest*, and if I'm lucky, maybe it will be, once this gets finished. She made a lot of special requests—carving, inlay—so hopefully I'll make it look good."

"It will be fantastic," Bell said, and he meant it. Chris was modest about his work, which was charming, especially compared to certain other people Bell had been forced to deal with today.

"Thanks. How was your day off? Do anything interesting?"

"Eehhh," Bell said, suddenly embarrassed. He didn't want to talk about how poorly his talk with DJ had gone. It seemed stupid now to have believed he could ever go back to that high-pressure world. "I did some work on my pitch for the dance studio. I have that meeting with Kathy tomorrow to discuss what exactly she needs, but I want to have some ideas to bring to the table. And I went out for lunch. The life of a pizza delivery boy isn't so exciting on his days off."

114

"Doesn't sound like it was too horrible," Chris said as he stepped back and brushed more sawdust from his clothes.

"The company could've been better."

"And how's that?" Chris asked.

"Well," Bell started, but Chris stepped back around to the other side of the armoire to put away his tools and tidy his work area. When Bell didn't continue, Chris prompted him with the wave of a hand.

"My mom called the other day and insisted I meet with this recruiter who is a friend of a friend of hers. I thought he might have some contract work-at-home-type stuff. But no. He was looking for the whole nine yards: long hours, schmoozing clients, travel, changing direction at the whim of anyone above me—which would be everybody."

Chris shrugged. "That sounds like typical corporate, but not *bad*."

"Oh, it gets worse. The recruiter was a total jackass. He was rude to the waitress and managed to insult the diner, the town, everyone else in the place, and my recent life choices in about three sentences. Impressive."

"Ah." Bell wished he could see Chris's face, but he was facing away from Bell. He sounded almost pleased, which was a bit odd—but maybe he was just happy Bell didn't plan to run off to the big city and Make Something of Himself.

"I'm lucky I escaped with my life," he said.

This time he *could* hear Chris laugh. "Poor baby. I'm glad you escaped the villain's clutches, but I'm sorry you had a trying day. Will dinner make it better?"

"Only if you're cooking."

"You can be sous chef," Chris allowed, and with one last clatter of tools against wood and plastic, he turned around. "Otherwise dinner could be a while. I had groceries delivered, but if you don't want to eat them raw, they'll need some prep."

"Pineville has grocery delivery?" Bell had looked for that service online when he first moved in, but he hadn't been able to find it.

"Betty at the corner shop offers it on certain days. Some of her customers can't carry heavy bags, so her husband drops off the bigger items."

"Wow. If she'd actually advertise that, I bet she'd be able to hire more delivery staff and still come out ahead." Bell stood up and stretched, which let him get a better look at Chris.

Chris grinned at him fondly and shook his head. "Okay, marketing boy wonder, think you can slow down the innovating to assist a simple country artisan?"

Bell sidled over to one of the sawhorses, leaned a hip into it, and struck a pose. "I might consider it for a hot meal and a quality benefits package." He gave Chris a long, obviously lascivious head-to-toe look.

"You're impossible, you know that?"

"Nah. Just statistically unlikely."

"Well, we'll see if you're still interested when I leave you to chop onions while I rinse the sawdust out of every crevice."

Now there was an arresting image. "Are you sure you wouldn't rather have help with *that*?"

"No," Chris said wryly. He shooed Bell toward the door. "You need anything from upstairs?"

"I'm good to go."

MUCH AS he claimed to be a hazard in the kitchen, Bell could actually handle chopping items as directed, and the use of a knife in close proximity with his fingers forced him to pay attention instead of daydream about Chris in the shower. He finished chopping the onion and then set it aside and contemplated the squash.

Chris had said he should cut it in half and peel it before chopping it. But cut it in half how? Peel it with what?

"Oh my God. Don't hurt yourself," Chris said from behind him. His hair stuck up in damp clumps, and his shirt clung to him again. Why couldn't he take three extra seconds to dry himself off properly and save Bell the embarrassing salivating?

"I was just waiting for some clarifications on this." Bell picked up the squash.

Chris pressed closer and hooked his chin on Bell's shoulder. "You've never cooked squash?" He reached for the knife and the squash, which boxed Bell in between Chris's arms, his body, and the counter. It wasn't a position very conducive to a cooking lesson.

"I could learn," Bell said. He'd massacre vegetables all night if it meant staying like this.

"Could, but won't." Chris kissed the side of his neck. Bell shivered at the tickle of his beard. "Snuggling and knife work… not a good pairing."

"No sense of adventure," Bell teased. Chris snorted, so Bell just angled his neck in a hint for another kiss. "I suppose I could make myself useful some other way."

"Useful would be better than distracting, if we want to eat any time tonight." Chris shifted away, and it was hard for Bell not to complain about the loss, even if he did want to tease Chris for being a hypocrite—the neck-kissing was his idea.

"Put me on drinks, then?"

"That sounds more like your wheelhouse." Chris softened the blow with a nudge of his hip. "Bottom shelf in the fridge. Should be a bottle of Grüner Veltliner."

"Oh, you do know how to impress." Bell fetched the wine and then fished around in the cutlery drawer for the corkscrew.

"Got to keep you coming back for something, don't I?"

Bell looked over from slicing the foil at the top of the bottle. "I don't know, I'm pretty hooked by now. You can probably stop trying so hard."

The picture of innocence, Chris raised his eyebrows—and the hand with the knife. "Oh, so you're saying I should just order pizza?"

"Maybe stop trying so hard *after* dinner," Bell amended. "No pizza outside working hours."

"I guess I'll have to do without a visit from the dashing Fred." Chris tried for a rueful expression as he returned to chopping.

Bell uncorked the wine and reached for the glasses. "It's not like he needs the extra tips on a weekend evening shift." He poured a taste into a glass that he held out for Chris, who shook his head. Bell took the taste instead and let the crisp, acidic flavor wash over his tongue. "That's delicious."

"What do you know. Even out here in the boonies, a guy can be classy enough to buy a decent wine that didn't even come in a box."

Chris's back was to him, so Bell couldn't see his face, but he didn't love the sound of Chris's voice.

Bell pursed his lips and put the glass down, taken aback. Sure, Chris ran hot and cold sometimes, but that reaction? Something more was going on. "Do you think I'm a snob?" he asked carefully. Suddenly he didn't feel so hungry.

Chris's posture stayed rigid even after he put down the knife. A few more seconds elapsed before he turned around, and Bell's heart pounded in his throat the whole time. He'd already done the whole song and dance with a college boyfriend who claimed Bell thought he was too good for him. He wasn't interested in doing that again.

He liked Chris a lot, but he needed them to be different.

Chris deflated like a sad balloon as soon as he saw Bell's face. "No, of course not. Come here." He opened his arms. Bell went, hesitantly at first, but melting into Chris was starting to come naturally. "I'm sorry. I had a lousy day and the most innocent things are getting to me right now. Maybe I should've come home alone."

Bell stiffened in Chris's arms, and not in the good way. "Should I go?" he said into Chris's shoulder. He would give Chris his space if he needed it, but he was really hoping Chris would ask him to stay.

"I'd rather you didn't, but I might not be the best company."

Bell might joke that Chris was definitely better than Lady Frances, but he didn't think that was what Chris needed to hear. "Even if you're cranky, there's no one else I'd like to spend the evening with." As soon as the words had left his mouth, Bell was afraid they were a little *too* true.

Damn it.

It must have been the right thing to say, though, because Chris drew back with a surprised almost smile and asked, tentative, "Really?"

Bell's ears burned, but he nodded. "Really. So. It sounds like we both had crummier-than-average days. Can we make dinner and drink this delicious wine—which, for the record, I would still drink if it were two-dollar boxed wine from Trader Joe's, because there's a time and a place for boxed wine—and then cuddle on the couch and pretend the rest of the day never happened?"

"I don't know. But I'm willing to give it a shot."

Finally Bell could relax, and he leaned forward and tucked his chin on Chris's shoulder. "Good. Let's try that again. Hey, Chris, I really like that wine you picked to go with dinner."

"Glad you like it. There's a professor in the agriculture department over at the college. I refinished an old bar for the basement that he turned into a wine cellar. I don't know which he liked more, the work or a chance to talk someone's ear off about wine. He's always coming by the shop with something he says I just have to try."

"Sounds like a good guy to know," Bell agreed. "And there seems to be a lot of that around."

"How so?" Chris threw the chopped vegetables in the pot.

"Everyone here has some sort of talent or interest that you might not expect, and they're all so eager to share it with everyone. Like your professor friend and his wine or the dance studio people who are all accountants or real estate agents or something. Jenny is going to start teaching a stained-glass workshop at the community center. I like it. Back home all that stuff got lost in the shuffle."

Chris smiled at first, but his expression took on a hint of horror as he added curry paste to the pot. "Oh God. I'm the quirky guy who makes dildos on the side." He reached for his wineglass and took a healthy swallow.

Bell laughed. "Yeah, I guess you are. Hey, so far I'm just the out-of-towner. At least you have something."

"You're not 'just' anything."

Oh, well, now they were getting somewhere. Bell's cheeks warmed. It could've been the wine. "Really? Tell me more."

"You're...." Chris sighed and drained his wineglass, then refilled it and topped up Bell's as well. He turned back to the pot and stirred the vegetables and curry more forcefully than Bell thought was strictly necessary. Then he poured in the chicken broth that had been warming on a back burner and put the lid on the pot. He didn't turn around right away.

"Chris?"

"Sorry," Chris said and turned back around. "Come on, let's go sit on the couch. The soup needs half an hour or so anyway." He held out his hand as they went into the other room.

Bell didn't like the way Chris was sitting almost an entire cushion away, so he slid down and leaned against Chris's shoulder. "You look worried. What's up?"

Blowing out a breath, Chris sagged deeper into the couch, taking Bell with him, whether by accident or design. "I saw you at the diner," he admitted, his tone somewhere between self-deprecating and annoyed. "And I've been stewing about it all day. I know it's irrational, and I'm trying not to be that jealous boyfriend you see on TV. But I really hate that guy, and I don't want him to take you away from me. Romantically or, you know, geographically."

Bell took that in, trying not to move too much lest he give his thoughts away. After a few seconds' deliberation, he offered, "That's simultaneously sweet and troublesome. I told you I'm into *you*. Remember?"

"Yeah, I remember." Chris leaned his head against Bell's. "Sorry."

Bell wrinkled his nose. "I'm not mad, just—wait. Did you say you know this guy?"

Chris waved his hand at the entertainment center. "We've talked about him before."

Bell sat up and turned around. ""DJ the appalling recruiter is also Derek your horrible ex with bad taste in home decorating?"

"Derek is his real name. DJ is an affectation he puts on for some nebulous business reason." Chris made a face that illustrated what he thought of that particular practice. "I'm pretty sure he didn't see me, and I'm also pretty sure he flirted with you."

"Well, he sure didn't pay much attention to my portfolio," Bell said as he curled back up against Chris. "He was more interested in how much money he could make headhunting me for this start-up marketing firm."

"I guess he left the job he had when we were together." Chris brushed his lips across Bell's forehead. "Thanks for not running off with my ex, even if it was just for work."

"Seriously," Bell said after a minute. "He is a horrible person. How did you even end up with him?"

There was a very significant pause. Then Chris said, sounding a little strangled, "Would you believe we met through work?"

"He *headhunted you*?" Bell almost screeched.

"Ow," Chris said. He raised a hand and rubbed his ear.

"Sorry. But seriously? Was that for the bank job that you completely hated?"

Chris squirmed underneath Bell's weight. "Maybe."

"*Ugh.*" Bell wanted a shower just talking about Chris *knowing* DJ. The idea that they'd been in a relationship—presumably a long and meaningful one—made his skin crawl. "So what happened? I mean, I assume he wasn't always as oily as he was at the diner. Because if so, you need higher standards."

"It wasn't like that, not at first. I don't know what happened. Well—" Chris made a face. "Lots of things… happened. Or didn't happen."

Warning alarms went off in Bell's head. That sounded ominous. "You moved here when your grandfather passed away, right? DJ said he lived in Pineville for a while."

"He didn't like that I quit the job he'd found me instead of taking the promotion. We tried to make it work after that, but…." He shrugged. "It was long over by then, I think, if I'm honest."

Bell wriggled around until he could see Chris's face but stay tucked under his arm. "Like you owed him for the job or something?"

"Not exactly," Chris said. "More like city mouse and small-town mouse. If I'd taken the promotion, the plan was to buy a nicer condo with a high-end kitchen, get a faster car, take fancier vacations to beaches with good party scenes."

"Pretty sure you'd blister within ten minutes," Bell said, reaching up to run his thumb along Chris's pale cheekbone. "Not to mention how bored you'd be."

Chris shrugged. "It's not that I am anti-money. I just want what I buy to have meaning, where DJ wanted to buy stuff that showed off what was in his bank account. Who needs more than one watch?"

"He was fixated on the diner pickles."

"They're made in-house. You tease me about being an artisan.... I think if we hadn't been together, he'd be the kind of guy who'd stop while driving through Pineville and then tell all his friends about the quaint woodworker he found in the hills. The artisan thing is trendy right now, so of course he likes the pickles. He's probably tried to get them into a magazine or something."

"I didn't like him," Bell said.

"I used to like him," Chris said, pulling Bell closer. "I was worried that you would too."

Something twigged at Bell's memory, and he huffed a tiny laugh. "He told me I should date his ex, actually, if you believe that. When I said I liked it here and had no intention of keeping up with the Joneses."

"He did not."

"He did," Bell said. He laughed harder at Chris's conflicted expression. "Only sensible thing he said the whole time. Other than ordering the pickles, of course."

"I don't know how I feel about that."

Sobering, Bell said, "I do," and slung himself into Chris's lap. "Your ex might be a pretentious sack of shit in designer clothing, but he got one thing right. I'm going to date the hell out of you."

Chris smiled as Bell touched their noses together. "Well, if you insist."

The kiss came as easy as breathing. Bell slipped into it between one second and the next, falling into the scrape of Chris's beard and the softness of his lips and the warmth of his body between Bell's thighs. Chris placed his hands just above the waistband of Bell's jeans and slid his thumbs under the hem of Bell's shirt. As they kissed,

Chris dragged the calloused pads of his thumbs over the soft skin there and made Bell shiver.

Chris pulled back a fraction. "You good?" he whispered against Bell's cheek.

"Mmm-hmm," Bell murmured. He didn't really want to stop kissing Chris, but verbalizing that he was all systems go, more than okay with this, was important. "More than good," he rasped. "You?"

Chris kissed him again in response, parted his lips under Bell's, and teased Bell's lower lip with his tongue as he walked his fingers up the back of Bell's shirt. Bell shivered in pleasure and let Chris in as his spine turned molten.

When the skin around his mouth started to burn from the abrasion of Chris's beard, Bell took a chance and broke for a breath. Then he kissed Chris's cheekbone and down toward his jawline. Beneath him, Chris inhaled sharply and dug his fingers in as if by reflex. Bell shivered again. Chris's hands spanned his rib cage, his thumbs tickling just under his pectoral muscles.

It felt strange to trail his lips along the edge of Chris's jaw, which was smooth near his ear and then interrupted with prickly hairs. They felt rougher against his lips than against his skin. He nuzzled at Chris's ear, then closed his lips on the lobe, kissing then tugging with his teeth. Chris groaned and slid his hands higher until his fingers teased just below Bell's nipples.

Bell made a soft sound and turned to kiss Chris again, more deeply, to encourage him. Chris picked up on the hint and made small, tight circles with his fingertips. In response Bell squeezed Chris's shoulders and shifted his hips. Chris's touch was firm enough to send spikes of pleasure through him but light enough to be a tease. Bell's jeans, as old and soft as they were, were going to be seriously uncomfortable very soon. He steadied himself with his hands on Chris's shoulders and desperately tried to keep himself from thrusting his hips.

Chris pinched his nipples lightly, and Bell lost that fight. He sucked Chris's lower lip into his mouth as his hips jerked forward without his permission. Chris made a small, sharp sound—not a protest—into his mouth and repeated the motion.

Bell's dick was so hard other parts of him were losing structural integrity. He sagged against Chris, kissing him frantically as he slid his fingers up into Chris's thick, soft ginger hair and scratched his nails over Chris's scalp. He forgot to be self-conscious, forgot to be careful. He wanted Chris closer.

Chris must have wanted that too, because he slid his hands down to Bell's hips again, lifted, and pushed—and suddenly Bell was lying on the couch with Chris pressed against him. Chris slotted his knee between Bell's thighs, making it impossible to resist the temptation to rock his hips. The kisses grew deeper and wetter, and Bell pulled away to catch his breath and to keep from getting too carried away. He finally had Chris against him, warm and responsive, and he didn't want it to end too quickly.

Bell turned away and arched his neck to inhale deeply, and Chris found the place right below his ear—first with his lips and then his teeth—and nipped at the skin over the tendon. Bell surprised himself with the sound he made, but Chris obviously wasn't taken aback as he redoubled his efforts at the sensitive spot.

Oh. Oh God. That felt good, and it had been so long since someone touched him like this. Heat tightened low in his stomach, and he breathed hard, almost dizzy. His dick was leaking, leaving a wet, slick trail on the inside of his boxers, and every time he shifted against Chris's thigh, the dampness smeared farther. The scent of Chris's shampoo—rosemary or something—filled his nose. He didn't know what it was, but he wasn't going to be able to smell it without getting a boner for the next who knew how long.

He should pull back. Were they moving too fast? Maybe they should talk about it. But his hands seemed to have a mind of their own, and they unthreaded from Chris's hair, moved down his firm chest, and only paused when they reached Chris's belt.

Chris scraped his teeth over that spot on Bell's neck, and Bell keened.

124

"Don't," Chris said a second later, hoarsely and almost too loud so close to Bell's ear. But before Bell could pull back, he continued. "Don't stop."

"Not stopping." Bell pulled the belt open, and Chris sighed when Bell unfastened the button of his jeans. When Bell tugged down his zipper, Chris recommitted himself to driving Bell crazy by scraping his teeth at the spot on his neck and scratching the tender skin with his beard. Bell was going to have obvious beard burn, and he was going to wear it proudly. He attempted to reach into Chris's boxers, but he bumped wrists with Chris, who was trying to return the favor. Bell's jeans were so old that he wished Chris could just rip into them, but the old button fly parted easily. Bell pushed his hips forward, shamelessly trying to press his cock into Chris's hand while he slipped his own hand into Chris's underwear.

Chris groaned as Bell wrapped a hand around his dick, and Bell smothered his own moan by mouthing at Chris's shoulder as he did the same. Chris was hot and thick in his hands. Bell flashed back to trying out the dildo and how he felt the shape and the weight of it and imagined this. The fantasy had been pretty great, but the reality was so much better, especially with Chris moving with him, giving Bell teasingly light touches, dragging his fingertips down his length. Bell thought to protest, to ask for more, but the slightly rough drag of skin on skin brought him up short. He doubted Chris was the type to stash lube between the sofa cushions, so they would have to improvise.

Bell closed his fingers around Chris's wrist and pulled his hand up to his face. Against his throat, Chris made a questioning noise and lifted his head, pulling back far enough that they made eye contact just as Bell sucked three of Chris's fingers into his mouth.

Chris's dick jerked in Bell's other hand and precome coated Bell's fingers. Bell licked and sucked and tasted a hint of himself on Chris's palm as he got him nice and wet. Chris's eyes were wide, his gaze riveted to Bell's mouth as Bell drew his teeth lightly over the pad of Chris's thumb.

Then Bell dragged Chris's hand back down, and Chris took the hint immediately. He smeared his thumb over the head of Bell's dick and then curled his fingers around him and stroked firmly but slowly. He dropped his head to Bell's neck again and dragged the side of his face against Bell's sensitive skin, making Bell curse and shudder.

A few more strokes and Bell had to let go of Chris's dick, because he was so close to coming he could taste it and he couldn't stop his hands from curling into fists. "God, Chris, that's really—" He faltered when Chris sucked just hard enough at the tendon below his ear.

Bell wanted more. He wanted Chris to play with his balls, wanted to see if he would take direction and finger Bell open. But with his jeans on, he didn't have room for more, and he didn't have time to ask for it anyway. As soon as Chris took that piece of skin between his teeth, Bell came, bucking helplessly into Chris's hand and clutching at the couch cushions because he was sure he was going to fuck himself right off of it. He was dimly aware of telling Chris how good it was, how good *he* was, or trying to, anyway. Coherent speech seemed out of reach.

What wasn't out of reach, figuratively or literally, was the hard length of Chris's cock as Bell composed himself enough to take it in his hand—which was very good, but Bell wanted to do better.

He needed Chris in a better position, though, so he had to do a little bit of cleanup first. He pulled his hand out of Chris's pants so he could grab Chris's wrist, and tugged it up. He murmured, "Got you, I've got you," at Chris's sounds of protest, which gave way to a surprised "ah" when Bell sucked Chris's slickened fingertips in his mouth. He flicked his gaze up to meet Chris's wide eyes. Bell slowly licked the taste of himself off Chris's hand and then dragged Chris's hand over his own T-shirt to take care of the rest. The tee's minutes were numbered anyway.

"Hey," Bell whispered against Chris's mouth. "Sit up for me?"

Chris grunted an acknowledgment, and Bell slipped off the couch as Chris got settled upright. Chris's plaid shirt hung open, and his cock, flushed and slick, stuck up out of the open slit of his boxers. Bell might have preferred them both naked, but disheveled was a seriously good look for Chris. Bell knelt on the floor and pushed Chris's knees apart. He peeled off his soiled tee and gave himself a quick swipe with it before tossing it aside. He stretched to show off a bit, hoping Chris appreciated the view. A glance up from under his eyelashes confirmed he had Chris's attention.

"I've been thinking about this a lot," he said as he bent down to get his mouth on Chris's dick.

"Oh," Chris said, sounding endearingly surprised. What did he think Bell planned to do on the floor? "Bell—" Chris's gratified-sounding groan provided further—if unnecessary—encouragement.

It had been a while, but Bell liked giving head, and he was already learning he was especially going to like doing it for Chris. He kept his mouth soft and wet as he mouthed at the tip and let his tongue take the salt-bitter flavor as he inhaled. Chris smelled like musk and herbal soap from his shower. Bell slid down to take more of him in. Chris groaned again, which was good, and then he put his hand in Bell's hair, and that was better. Bell hummed in encouragement, bobbing his head, and got Chris's other hand on his shoulder, which was perfect. He was surrounded by the bracket of Chris's thighs and the warm strength of his hands, and his mouth was full of him. It didn't get better than this.

Except it did, of course. When Bell concentrated he could hear Chris's heavy breathing over the wet sounds from his own mouth. And the longer Bell sucked him, the wetter he got, until Bell lost himself in the slick rhythmic slide.

Chris's hips stuttered beneath Bell's palms when Bell pushed himself deeper, and Chris cursed even as he loosened his sudden death grip on Bell's shoulder. "Sorry, sorry. Rude," he gasped, and his thigh muscles trembled against Bell's shoulders.

Bell almost wanted to ask how long it had been since anyone did this for Chris, but that would be a definite mood killer. Instead he concentrated on making sure Chris would remember this experience for years to come.

Rather than responding to Chris's apology, he moved his right hand to cover Chris's on his shoulder and squeezed gently. Then he coaxed him to move it over so his fingers curled around Bell's nape, giving him implicit permission.

"Fuck," Chris said as Bell fluttered his tongue just under the crown and watched Chris with hooded eyes.

Chris watched him back with his mouth slack and his face flushed. His regard made Bell feel hot all over, from his tingling, pebbling nipples down to his balls and beyond, and his cock twitched hopefully.

One thing at a time, Bell told himself firmly. Then he lapped the head of Chris's dick and took him as deep as he could.

Chris made an inhuman sound and tugged sharply at Bell's hair. "Gonna make me come," he panted.

That was the goal. Bell pulled his mouth off Chris's dick and took over with his hand. His grip slid easily through spit and precome. Chris let out one more aborted cry and came hot and sticky over Bell's fingers. He splashed Bell's chest and even dripped down onto Bell's jeans. Bell stroked until Chris shuddered and twitched minutely away, and then he sat back and took in the mess they'd made.

Or, well. They'd *made* the mess together, sure. But somehow Chris had escaped relatively unscathed, while Bell had spit drying on his face and come clumping in the thin line of peach fuzz that led down from his navel. And while that was really hot in the moment, now it was just kind of gross.

He retrieved his shirt from the floor to mop himself up and then kicked it away. It definitely wasn't fit to be worn again without washing. Bell would have to depend on Chris to lend him something to wear home. And, well… when he thought of going home, he felt unsure of the etiquette. Was a blow job on the couch something Chris would want to follow up with cuddling, or was Bell supposed to make a graceful, if topless, exit?

His thoughts were interrupted by a rumble from Chris's stomach and then an embarrassed chuckle.

"Try to consider that a compliment?" Chris smiled down at Bell and reached out to haul him back up. He was flushed and a little sweaty, and Bell leaned in for a kiss. Chris pulled him in, and Bell took care not to put a knee anywhere vulnerable. He settled down, half in Chris's lap, and was happy to find that, yes, Chris was a cuddler and a very good one. He leaned them both back into the corner of the couch, chest to chest, heedless of the stickiness still clinging to Bell. Chris would have to do laundry too.

"What part is the compliment, exactly?" Bell asked, a little smug but also a little addled as he idly ran his hand down Chris's chest. Next time he was going to get Chris's shirt off, for sure. "The part where you came all over me or the rumbling stomach?"

A sudden silence fell, and Bell tilted his head up and met Chris's embarrassed eyes. As one they turned toward the kitchen. "How long did you say the soup was supposed to cook?" Bell asked carefully.

For another second neither of them moved. Then they scrambled up almost at the same time, half tripping as they got their jeans untangled from around their legs.

Chris beat Bell into the kitchen by half a second. The soup was bubbling madly on the stove, and orange-red splashes dotted the counter and cooktop. The kitchen window had steamed up, but nothing seemed to be on fire.

Chris turned the burner to low and grabbed a dishtowel. Bell almost remarked that they should just declare splattered messes the theme of the evening, but he decided to go for the safer "Soup is better the longer it goes, yeah?"

"That's the theory," Chris muttered as he gave it another stir. "Can you grab a few—" Chris turned to face Bell and grinned sheepishly. "I was going to say grab some bowls, but I think you're not dressed for dinner."

"Fancy place you got here, mister." Bell grinned back. "No shirt, no shoes, no soup?"

Chris snorted and swatted his towel playfully at Bell. "Hot soup spills are no joke. Get the bowls, and I'll go get you something to put on."

Chris disappeared into the back of the house while Bell washed up and set the table with spoons and napkins. The shirt Chris brought out was a soft gray Henley that smelled a little like Chris's detergent and a bit like cedar. Bell hoped Chris wouldn't be asking for it back anytime soon. He smiled as he pulled it on. "Thanks."

Chris donned an apron for the final step, because it involved taking an immersion blender to the soup and spattering curry-scented squash everywhere. That would probably stain like crazy, but it smelled amazing. And when Chris ladled it into the bowls and garnished it with crème fraîche and pumpkin seed oil, it looked—well, not *better*, but equally as delicious. "What do you think?" Chris asked as Bell took his first taste.

The soup was perfect—thick, hot, fragrant, creamy, a little nutty. Bell swallowed his mouthful, licked his lips, and stared at his bowl. It was probably too soon to ask for seconds. "Well, it still would've been worth it if we'd wrecked it, but it would've been a shame."

Chris flushed, obviously pleased with the double compliment. "It's my grandmother's recipe. Well, sort of. She used different spices, but the base is the same."

Bell smiled. Knowing Chris had made him a family recipe, however modified, gave him the warm fuzzies. "It's really good." He quirked one corner of his mouth up. "Did you grow the squash yourself?"

"Not this time. Grandma always did, though. Maybe next year."

Bell had a sudden flash of the two of them in the garden patch in Chris's backyard in the summer, digging in the soft loam and pulling weeds—whatever vegetable gardening entailed. He didn't have more than a vague idea, but he looked forward to finding out.

Then again, it seemed impossible that Chris would manage to find time for gardening, his extensive home-renovation hobby, work, *and* Bell. But Bell pushed that thought aside.

By the time they finished dinner, Bell's eyelids were heavy. Fighting off an impolite yawn, he helped Chris load the dishes into the dishwasher and put away the leftovers.

"You look tuckered out," Chris said and ruffled Bell's hair. "Do you want to crash here, or should I run you home?"

Bell leaned forward, just enough to feel Chris's warmth. "Would you mind if I stayed?"

"Of course not," Chris said. "It's the sofa or bunking in with me, though—your pick."

"Who's going to snuggle me if I sleep on the sofa?"

Chris laughed. "Intruders and ghosts, mostly. You'd be safer in my bed."

"Then me being in your bed is clearly the right decision," Bell said, slipping a hand into Chris's back pocket and squeezing lightly.

"The price is you helping me change the sheets," Chris said after a moment, his cheeks flushed pink with apparent embarrassment. "I'm just glad I have clean ones that aren't my old *Star Wars* set."

"I am not entirely sure you're joking," Bell said.

Chris grinned at him and kissed his forehead. "You may never know."

"Oh no," Bell said and tugged Chris toward the bedroom. "You have a linen closet, and I'm going through it."

Unfortunately for Bell the linen closet didn't yield any vintage textiles bearing R2-D2 or Chewbacca, but it did cough up a nice bamboo cotton set that felt incredibly soft, which would have to do until Bell could undertake a more thorough search. He and Chris got the bed habitable with a minimum of verbal communication, and Bell was all set to just crawl in and pass out, until he took his jeans off and remembered his boxers had also been a victim of his own libido, if not to the same extent as his shirt.

It probably wasn't polite to get in fresh sheets wearing less-than-fresh underwear.

Before he could open his mouth to ask, Chris cleared his throat, and Bell looked over to see him blush and shrug sheepishly. "Do you want a quick shower and something to wear to bed?"

The prospect of hot water did sound tempting. "You going to join me?"

"If I did, it'd only be to keep you from drowning yourself." Chris opened a drawer in the dresser and took out a pair of boxers. "Towels in the cupboard."

At Chris's direction, Bell took the clean boxers and dirty sheets into the bathroom and ran the hot water until the room filled with steam. He stripped out of the shorts he was wearing and threw them into Chris's hamper, along with the sheets. He hoped that he wasn't crossing some sort of relationship line, but it was better than leaving them on the floor.

A few bottles stood on a tiled corner shelf in the shower, and Bell took each one down to sniff it. The shampoo smelled warm, like the wood shavings in the shop, while the bath gel smelled like oranges and cloves. The scents made him wonder if Chris was already tucked up under the covers, reading something by lamplight. Or was he curled around a pillow, half-asleep? Bell wasn't sure whether sleep or something more active was on the agenda, but he'd use up all the hot water if he didn't turn off the shower.

He got out, toweled off, and pulled on Chris's boxers. Then he opened the door and went to sit on the bed next to Chris. "Hey. I like your shower stuff."

"Me too," Chris said. He took off his glasses and put them on the bedside table. "Do you have a side preference?"

"Oh, do I get a whole side to myself? Lady Frances is a bed hog."

"You're letting her get away with too much, then."

"Hey, until today she was the most company I've had in my bed in a long time. But I basically sleep wherever she doesn't, so…. Do *you* have a side preference?" On second thought the answer was pretty obvious when he bothered to look around. Chris's glasses and an alarm clock sat on one night table, while the other remained unadorned except for a fine layer of dust. It was most likely from all of the home renovations and not because Chris neglected his housekeeping. "Never mind. I think I answered my own question."

Chris made an inarticulate noise as Bell climbed over him to the other side of the bed. "It's not that I'm a completely awful housekeeper, but—"

"But you're remodeling," Bell said as he punched his pillow into shape. "If everything were dust-free and perfect, you'd either be done with remodeling, or you'd be the most uptight person in Pineville."

"It's something I've heard before," Chris said as he switched off the light.

"We are not talking about DJ right before falling asleep." Bell grabbed Chris's hips and pushed him into place so Bell could spoon against him. "I am not interested in having an anxiety dream in your bed, okay?"

"Okay," Chris said, and he flipped Bell so that Chris became the big spoon.

Bell looked over his shoulder and frowned. "I knew you were in shape, but I didn't know you were that strong. Woodworking is a better resistance workout than I thought."

"Nah. I went to college on a sports scholarship," Chris said as he nuzzled Bell's neck at the hairline. "Now hush and go to sleep. Some of us have to work in the morning." He slid a hand around Bell's waist and flatted his palm against Bell's stomach.

With Chris tucked against him, warm and cozy, Bell had another thought of bedroom activities that didn't involve sleep. But it had been a long, trying day, and Chris's mattress already had Bell under its spell. "Okay," he agreed and closed his eyes. "But next time I get to be big spoon." Someone had to ensure that Chris received his share of physical comfort, and Bell was willing to make that sacrifice.

He felt Chris's lips pull into a smile against the back of his neck. "Deal."

CHAPTER TEN

BELL WOKE hungry, half-hard, and alone.

At first when he knuckled the sleep from the corners of his eyes, he was too busy being hopeful about the second thing to register the third. Then he blinked and his eyes adjusted to the morning light, and he saw that the room was empty. Chris was gone from the bed, the covers tucked carefully back in around Bell.

Well. At least Bell's boyfriend spared a thought for his comfort while fleeing what should have been a cozy morning after.

Bell closed his eyes again and pressed his face into the pillow, which didn't help. His hair had still been damp when he went to bed, and the pillowcase smelled like Chris's shampoo. Surely Chris wasn't so dense as to think this was acceptable first-sleepover behavior, right? Bell was going to get whiplash from the mixed signals.

Even though he was tempted, Bell knew he couldn't stay curled up in Chris's bed feeling sorry for himself. He got up, tucked in the sheets, and tugged the quilt into place as best he could. After a quick visit to the bathroom, where he failed to make his hair behave, he pulled on his jeans and the Henley Chris had loaned him the night before, and went to the kitchen.

A travel mug sat on the countertop, next to a plate covered with a clean dishtowel. Bell pulled the dishtowel off to find two blueberry muffins, still warm. He took the mug and plate to the table, where he found a house key sitting on top of a note.

Sorry I had to leave so early. It was hard not to wake you up. Good luck with your meeting today!

Chris had even signed his name, as though Bell was going to get confused by all the guys who might leave him muffins and a cup of coffee exactly the way Bell liked it—in Chris's kitchen, no less.

Bell was starting to feel like he was dating several different people, and one of them was still living in the Victorian age. He thought he could maybe do without that particular aspect of Chris's personality, but that was probably the one who left Bell fresh baked goods. And after their night together, Bell felt optimistic that there was a horndog in there, somewhere. Finding him might take time, but Bell could handle the challenge.

Especially if he got muffins in the meantime.

He took a picture of his plate, entirely devoid of crumbs, captioned it with a *<3*, and sent it to Chris as a thanks. But he couldn't let go of the fact that he'd rather have woken up with Chris than breakfast, so he sent another message right afterward. *Your muffins are great, but fyi for next time id rather have a protein shake.*

It might be a little too honest, but picking up on subtlety wasn't Chris's strong suit.

He put the plate in the dish drainer and then locked himself out of the house with his unconventionally acquired house key. It was a crisp, sunny morning, and the last bits of frustration melted away as he walked home.

When Bell let himself into the shop, he could hear voices from the back. It wasn't clear whether Chris had been expecting customers or if it was a drop-in, but either way, Bell wouldn't interrupt. He needed to get ready for his meeting with Kathy anyway, and it wasn't polite to eavesdrop on Chris at work, even if he was wildly curious about who Chris thought was more important than snuggling with his cute boyfriend.

Before Bell had a chance to close the apartment door, he heard Chris's voice.

"Drop it, Will. You've already given me enough grief about *not* dating, and now you're on me about actually doing it?"

That just wasn't fair. How was Bell supposed to do the right thing now, especially when his landlord apparently had opinions on Bell's private life?

"I'm not *on you*, Chris. This isn't an intervention. I just worry that you're moving too fast. Your track record—"

"Can we not talk about DJ, please? Preferably ever"—Bell privately agreed. The less oxygen wasted on DJ, the better—"but especially not this morning. I was in a good mood."

Bell allowed himself a heartbeat to feel a little smug. He imagined Chris downstairs feeling much the same, and felt even more smug.

"Really," Will said, his tone full of suspicion. "*How* good?"

Yeah, Chris, how good? Bell's ears were burning, but before he could hear anything else, Lady Frances appeared from seemingly out of nowhere and trotted primly down the stairs.

"Hey, girl," Will said, a moment later. "Where did you come from? Come tell me what's going on, since Chris isn't giving me any help."

Bell heard Lady Frances chirp a greeting in return. Apparently she liked Will just fine too.

"She shouldn't be down here," Chris said. "She usually hangs out in the apartment unless—hold on."

Before Bell could pretend to be busy with all the things he needed to take to his meeting, Chris's steps sounded on the stairs and he appeared in the doorway. "I didn't know you were here," he said, his face flushed.

"Just got here," Bell said. "I didn't want to intrude on your conversation."

"I wasn't expecting him," Chris said. "But I haven't really expected Will for the past fifteen years, so this isn't new."

Bell grabbed the fabric of Chris's overshirt and pulled him closer. "You can explain this all to me later, but the man does have a point. Just how good of a mood were you in this morning?"

"Good enough to put up with my best friend's meddling," Chris said and brushed a kiss across Bell's forehead. "You should probably come downstairs before—"

"Before what?" Will stood just inside Bell's open apartment door with Lady Frances curled in his arms. She had a satisfied look on her face. And even though Bell had met Will before, he couldn't help a double-take. He looked like something straight out of *GQ*. Bell had never seen stubble so perfect, or eyebrows so well groomed… or anyone else in town with that much fashion sense, if he were completely honest. Where had the tweed gone?

"Before he takes matters into his own hands and invites himself into your apartment," Chris finished dryly, apparently unaffected by Will's extreme hotness. Bell panicked for a second, trying frantically to remember if he'd left one of Chris's dildos out in an incriminatingly obvious location. "Bell, you've met Will Kettering, landlord. *This* is Will Kettering, my very old, very nosy friend. Will, this is Bell. My boyfriend."

"I am a grand total of seventeen hours older than you," Will said. Bell got the feeling they'd had this argument a time or twelve. "Your boyfriend, on the other hand. If I didn't know better, I'd think he picked you up at the college."

"Hey," Bell protested, sure he'd been insulted.

Chris rolled his eyes. "As if I could set foot on campus without you knowing about it, you busybody."

Lady Frances *mrrowl*ed and jumped neatly from Will's arms to twine around Bell's ankles in a pointed reminder.

Bell removed his hands from Chris's shirt and went to satisfy Lady Frances's hungry demands. He wasn't going to get into whatever this was between Chris and Will, at least until he figured out what was actually going on.

"Sue me for caring about you," Will said. He crossed his arms and glared at Chris.

Ah.

"I know you care," Chris said. "You had to pick up the pieces after DJ, and that sucked for you, and I will appreciate you until the day one of us drives the other crazy."

Will shrugged and sat down on the edge of Bell's bed. "I don't like it when you're sad."

"Me neither," Chris said. "But can we not drag all my laundry out in front of Bell? I mean, he's already met DJ. I don't want him to think I'm all drama and bad choices."

Will's jaw dropped, and he stared at Bell. "You've met DJ?"

"Unfortunately," Bell said. "A friend of my mom's uses him as a headhunter. She gave him my e-mail and, for some disturbing reason, a photo of me."

"Imagine my surprise," Chris said dryly, "when I stopped into the diner for pancakes and found my ex eating pickles in a booth with my boyfriend."

"I hope you grabbed the coffeepot and poured it on his crotch," Will said.

"If only. Then I wouldn't have had to listen to him condescend at me for forty minutes." Bell made a face and set Lady Frances's dish on the floor. "But I'll definitely keep that in mind for next time."

When he stood up again, Will was watching him through narrowed eyes. "You weren't taken in by his good looks and charm and promise of a life of luxury?" He put a sarcastic emphasis on *charm*.

Apparently Will had known DJ well, though Bell found it ironic that he was picking on DJ's good looks when Will was easily the most attractive human Bell had ever laid eyes on in person. "I left a high-paying job as a junior consultant to be a vagabond and then became a pizza boy." He struggled with telling people that, sometimes, as though they might judge him the way his parents would, so he made sure it came out as a challenge.

Chris must have picked up on Bell's edginess, because he stepped between them. "Is that enough now? Can you lay off, please?"

Will remained nonplussed. "No, sorry. One more question." Except then he turned to Chris. "Did you leave him in bed this morning to wake up alone?"

"Yes," Chris said after a moment. "And it was a stupid decision, but it's not your business to chew me out, and you know why I did it."

Will sighed and stood up, pulling Chris into a hug. "If I ever run into that guy…." He finally let Chris go and turned to Bell. "If you need help interpreting Chris at any point, come find me. I have experience."

"Shut *up*," Chris said. "And thank you."

Will grinned and slapped him on the back. "Hey, you helped me land the prettiest girl in all of Canada. I figure I owe you a little something." He looked at his watch. "I'm almost late for soccer, though. Bell, you play?"

"It's been a while," Bell said.

"I keep trying to get Chris to put his cleats back on, but so far no luck." Will shrugged and bent to pet Lady Frances and then waved as he went downstairs. "Nice seeing you again."

Bell and Chris stayed quiet until they heard the jingle of the front door's bells. "That wasn't exactly a shovel speech," Bell said. "Maybe one of those little hand shovels that people use in the garden?"

"A trowel," Chris said. "That was definitely a trowel speech. Will's not threatening enough to reach shovel levels of intimidation."

Bell hooked his fingers into Chris's front jeans pockets. "I don't know. His eyebrows are perfect enough to intimidate all by themselves, and does he measure his stubble or something?"

Chris laughed, though he didn't make eye contact with Bell. "He's always looked like that, even in college, when all the guys on the team dyed their hair blond."

"Even you?"

"Even me," Chris said. "But I cut it with Will's beard trimmer as soon as the red started to grow back in."

"Pictures, please." Bell pulled Chris closer. "You don't have to tell me what's going on if you don't want to, and thank you for the muffins. But if there's something I really do need to know, can I count on you telling me?"

Chris dropped his head to rest on Bell's shoulder. "Yeah," he said. "I just worry you're going to figure out I'm a crotchety old man in the making. As soon as I get all that crabgrass out of my lawn, I'm going to start telling kids to get off of it, and then spend the evening ranting about how television isn't what it used to be."

"Maybe I like cranky guys in cardigans and ancient jeans who yell at World War II documentaries," Bell said, kissing the shell of

Chris's ear. "Maybe I just like you. Tell me more about you and Will and the hair dye?"

"Not right now," Chris said. "I wanted to ask if I can make it up to you about this morning, if you'll let me."

"I'm good with that," Bell said, then frowned and pulled out his phone. "But I have to be at the dance studio in an hour, and I'm not done with my presentation yet."

"I meant later anyway. I've got to pack up a big order of bowls to take to the handcraft gallery." Chris bounced his forehead lightly against Bell's shoulder. "I keep forgetting you haven't been here very long. I just kind of assume you know my schedule."

"Wake up, work, drink coffee, work, fuss at your ledger, mentor Chloe, work some more, order pizza, banter with Joseph, flirt with the pizza guy, work all afternoon, refuse to play soccer with your best friend, then start cooking an amazing dinner for your boyfriend but get interrupted by blow jobs?"

"That mostly sounds perfect," Chris murmured, and he gave Bell a soft and lingering kiss. "Please keep putting up with me."

"Same," Bell said as he mouthed along Chris's jaw. "But you should really start playing soccer with Will so I can watch your ass in soccer shorts."

"I'll keep that in mind." Chris kissed him again, though this time it was hard and brief. "We can either stand here and make out until we miss our appointments, or we can get some work done and have the evening free."

Bell was about to pull Chris in again when his phone chimed. "Damn it. That was my forty-five-minute warning. You have to go away now or I'll be penniless and living on mistake pizza for the rest of my life, freeloading off my handsome man."

"Will's already married," Chris said, tapping Bell's nose.

"Good, I'd hate to have to compete with him." Bell did pull away this time, with one last peck on the lips. He made it up to himself by reaching around to smack Chris's butt to send him on his way. "Now get out of here."

Chris left, and Bell, after watching his ass as he went down the first few stairs, took out his laptop and typed furiously into a template document to get down everything that had been percolating in his head for the past few days. He printed a couple copies of a generic contract—one he could fill in the numbers on before they signed, depending on what Kathy wanted and could afford—and a few blank quote sheets. He had a good feeling, and he wanted to be prepared.

By the time he'd finished everything he wanted to do before the appointment, he only had a few minutes to change into something remotely professional and no time left over to shave. Unfortunately stubble didn't look quite as good on him as it looked on Will, but it was too late to do anything about it. Bell put his laptop in his computer bag, slid his papers into the protective folder, put on his uncomfortable dress shoes, and was out the door.

He made it to the studio with moments to spare. Kathy met him at the office door, dressed in leggings, leg warmers, and a baggy T-shirt. She had a sweatband ostensibly keeping sweat off her face, though it mostly acted as a magnet for stray wisps of damp hair. "Hey, Bell. Sorry about the…." She gestured to encompass her current state. "I had to fill in unexpectedly. One of our DanceFit instructors got the flu. 'Tis the season."

For a second Bell didn't quite understand what she meant. Then he realized it was November and he'd somehow been living his new life in Pineville for a month and a half.

Huh. "I guess it is," he said. "But it's no big deal to me. Unless you'd rather reschedule?"

"No, let's do it now. Who knows when I'll have another chance if someone else gets sick." Kathy pulled a towel from a bookshelf and wiped it over her face. Then she draped it over the office chair and sat down. "So, first things first. How much are you going to cost me? I don't want to be rude, but if I can't afford you, I figure it's better not to waste either of our time."

Bell blinked and then shook it off and pulled out a quote sheet. "That's the thing about working for yourself. You can be a little flexible. I came up with a couple different packages at various price points. Though if you're having major budgetary problems, I can also consult on that, help you find ways to cut expenses. Um, depending how in-depth I'd need to go, that's one of the more expensive services I can offer."

"Let's talk about the marketing strategy pricing first," Kathy said, looking a little overwhelmed. Bell wasn't surprised. Most people needed time to ease themselves into the sort of mindset where they were willing to change that much.

Nodding, Bell pulled out his laptop and went over the packages. "None of these are set in stone—if you want to swap different things, like building a social-media platform versus a website, or something, I can price that out too."

They poked and prodded until Kathy found a package she liked at a price the studio could afford, and once they had the paperwork signed, Bell pulled up his list of proposals.

Kathy raised her eyebrows. "Just like that? You were awfully sure I was going to hire you if you spent all those hours on it."

"I have a lot of free time," Bell said sheepishly. "My boyfriend has a project house." Then he shrugged. "Besides, if you were on the fence, I could've used this stuff to win you over. Now let's talk promotions. Christmas is coming, and New Year's means New Year's resolutions...."

BELL WOULD have been perfectly happy to conclude his Saturday by working up a few of the things he'd talked about with Kathy into strategies he could implement as soon as possible, all while sitting in the chair he'd claimed as his in Chris's workshop. Sure, he'd rather have been upstairs having his way with Chris or at Chris's canoodling on the couch, but he'd known what he was signing up for, and he had plenty to keep him busy. Besides, simply spending time in Chris's presence made him feel relaxed and welcome and... whatever the antonym of *alone* was. Not a bad way to spend a Saturday afternoon and evening. He even tiptoed upstairs just before six and put together some sandwiches and cut veggies for dinner. Chris probably would've made his own bread or something, but he still looked up with a sweet, pleased, surprised expression when Bell cleared his throat and handed him a plate. Bell's insides went pleasantly warm.

Oh wow. This was serious.

But before he could get too lost in that thought, Chloe came in from whatever errand Chris had sent her on. When Chris mumbled something about needing to go place an order, she gave his retreating form a furtive glance and then rolled a stool over next to Bell.

"Hey," she said.

Uh-oh. Bell smelled shenanigans. "Hi?"

"So you and the boss man had a date last night, huh?"

Jesus. "I don't think that's any of your business," Bell tried.

"Relax, I don't want any gross details." Chloe rolled her eyes. "Old people. Ugh." While Bell was still trying to work out whether to be offended—either on Chris's behalf or his own—she continued. "It was just an introductory comment for my true agenda."

He shook his head. "By all means carry on."

Chloe scooted closer and grasped his arm, her expression imploring. "Make him take weekends off."

If only. Bell managed a small smile. "I'll work on it."

Five minutes later he was still digesting his epiphany—and the sandwich, and his unease about Chloe's request—when his phone rang with the Imperial March.

Chris looked up from marking a cut. "Did you change your mother's ringtone?"

"You can't prove anything," Bell said, sulking, and Chris laughed as Bell answered the phone. "Hi, Mom."

"Hi, honey," his mom answered, sounding cheerful as always. "I just called to ask how the interview went. That was yesterday, right?"

As if she'd forget. Bell winced and resigned himself to more half-truths. "It was fine," he said. "The recruiter seemed... interested."

"Oh," she said. She sounded almost surprised. Then she recovered. "Well, did you call him to follow up? You know how much employers appreciate people who take initiative."

Suddenly Bell had the distinct impression that his mother already knew the gist of what had happened yesterday, though filtered through DJ and Elaine and colored with DJ's prejudice, to boot. "No," he said.

"Oh," his mom said. She sounded tentative and confused. "Bellamy, you know that if you want this job—"

"I don't, though," Bell burst out, so sharply that Chris looked up from his tape measure and cocked his head in apparent concern. Bell shook his head, and he went back to his work.

"What? Honey, I appreciate that you want to make your own way, but I'm just not sure self-employment is really stable enough to support you—"

"This is not up for discussion, Mom," Bell snapped. When he accidentally met Chris's gaze again, Chris blushed but quickly returned his attention to the task in front of him. Bell should probably leave so Chris didn't feel like he was eavesdropping, but the conversation was a lot easier with Chris there. "When and if I decide to reconsider, it will be just that—my decision. But it won't involve Elaine's friend DJ, who is a stuck-up, narcissistic twat if I've ever met one."

"Bellamy Alexander!"

"Well, he is." Bell refused to apologize for sticking up for himself for once in his life. If he did that, she'd soon have him promising to call DJ back and grovel. He wouldn't do it. "Was there something else you wanted to talk about, Mom?" *Or did you just call to nag about my career?*

His mother inhaled an audible breath. "As a matter of fact, I wanted to ask when you were planning on coming home for Thanksgiving so I could make sure I have everything ready. You are staying with us, right?"

Shit. "Thanksgiving?" Bell echoed weakly.

Across the room Chris looked up, met Bell's gaze, and then quickly looked away again.

"It's only two weeks away," his mom reminded him. Fuck. That was soon. Bell couldn't believe he'd forgotten. He hadn't even thought to bring it up with Jenny and Antonio. He didn't know if the restaurant was open and he'd be expected to deliver pizzas as usual. "Do you think you can make it up on Wednesday? We miss having you around."

Awesome. She was laying on the guilt. As if they'd seen him that often when he lived nearby and they all worked eighteen-hour days. Except Mom, of course, who'd become a career society wife once Bell started middle school. But she'd spent far more time on the tennis court than with them. "I'm not sure about my work schedule yet," he said truthfully. "I'll let you know."

"Schedule? I thought you were freelancing."

Bell tried to take a measured breath. "I am, but it's complicated." He grasped at straws, anything he could say to get his mother off his case. Then he realized she'd given him the perfect excuse. "You know what it's like setting up your own business. The first few months are crucial. I need to get established."

"Of course, honey. I didn't think of that. But I understand." Bell breathed an internal sigh of relief. "I'm still disappointed, of course. You'll try to make it?"

"I'll try," Bell said. "No promises."

He endured a few more minutes of small talk and then begged off with the excuse that he had work to do—which, technically, he did. Then he hung up and tried to get his chair to swallow him whole.

No such luck.

"So how are things with Mom?" Chris asked dryly.

"Don't start," Bell groaned and sat up. Did Chris have plans for Thanksgiving? Were they supposed to do that sort of thing together? Or was their relationship too new to warrant parental introductions? Chris's parents lived halfway across the country anyway. In all likelihood they wouldn't be visiting, and Chris would have mentioned if he were going to see them. "I'm not sure I have the patience to field her questions in person."

"Poor baby."

Bell stuck his tongue out at him, then gave in to his curiosity and asked, "What are your plans for Thanksgiving, by the way? You haven't mentioned."

"Dinner with Will and Kristine and maybe their parents. I'm not sure exactly who's coming. Sometimes Will adopts a TA or two for a semester. I'm sure you're more than welcome too, though I can't promise Kristine will ask fewer questions than your mom."

"Probably not, if she's as protective of you as her husband." They were different kinds of questions, though. Bell didn't mind answering questions about Chris. His intentions were pure... in a manner of speaking. And he thought it would probably do Chris some good to overhear Bell gushing about how in like he was.

He got the feeling Will would totally set him up for some good ego boosting too.

"It's not the same as spending the holidays with family, though, so I'd understand if you can't make it."

Something about that sounded not quite right, but Bell couldn't put his finger on it, so he let it slide. "I don't even know if I have Thanksgiving off yet. But I'll let you know." Even if he couldn't make it home for the day itself, he generally had three-day weekends. He could leave after work on Thursday or early on Friday, visit his family all day Saturday, and return Sunday.

But even without the nosy-mom factor, he'd much rather spend the weekend with Chris—even though he spent more or less every weekend with him. Of course Chris was usually working....

A loud yawn interrupted his thought process, and he looked up and narrowed his eyes. "Okay, no more power tools for you."

Chris gave him a sheepish look. "You may have a point."

"I absolutely have a point. I like you with all your bits attached. Not that I wouldn't still—" Bell bit down on what he'd been about to say and tried to cover with a shake of his head. He didn't know if he succeeded. He was too busy being surprised. "I just want you to be safe. No impaired judgment while operating heavy machinery."

"I promise," Chris said solemnly. Then he blinked. "Am I allowed to drive myself home?"

Bell had hoped he might want to stick around and make up for leaving Bell alone in bed that morning, but he looked beat, and he'd basically been at work for twelve hours. Bell couldn't fault him for wanting to go to sleep. Besides, Bell had his own work to keep him occupied for a bit longer. They could relax together tomorrow. "I'll let it slide this once, but next time you're sleeping over." He paused. "And no sneaking out in the morning."

Chris smiled and shook his head. "I promise to stay *and* make you breakfast."

Bell was thinking more along the lines of blow jobs in bed, but never mind. "It's a start," he said, helpless to do anything but smile back. "Now go before you fall asleep."

Before he left, Chris leaned down and planted a soft, sweet kiss on Bell's mouth. "Good night."

"Good night," Bell said. He stayed in his chair as the lights in the rest of the shop went dark, until the only one remaining lit the stairway to his apartment.

Then he slithered down against the cushion and raised his hand helplessly to his lips.

CHAPTER ELEVEN

BELL SPENT Sunday in a dance-studio-marketing haze, exchanging only a handful of texts with Chris. He was intent on finishing the prep work so he could meet a publication deadline for the college newspaper, which went to print on Tuesday. On Monday morning, when he emerged from the other side of the blitz, he felt too stupid to do much more than put some food in a bowl for Lady Frances. But he could hear Chris puttering about downstairs, so odds were good he could score some coffee. Bell shoved on a pair of shoes, grabbed a clean mug, and shambled into the shop.

"Good morning," Chris said from his office as Bell walked past the open door. He stopped just to poke his head in, but Chris got up to wrap Bell in a loose embrace and press a quick kiss against his mouth. Bell should have brushed his teeth, probably. He blinked and tried not to lean too obviously into Chris's chest, but he was so nice and warm and his shirt was soft. Bell wanted to rub his face on Chris's beard. Or vice versa. One of these days, Bell was going to get him to sleep in and cuddle.

Maybe.

"Hi," he said back, a beat or two late. Then he held up his mug hopefully. "Coffee?"

Chris chuckled and spun him around to face the showroom and its coffeemaker. "Coffee," he promised, nudging Bell forward. "Productive day yesterday?"

"I finished," Bell said proudly. He let Chris take the mug from his hands, fill it, and then pass it back. "I'm going to remember this for next year. Pre-Thanksgiving marketing crunch." If he had more than two clients, he'd start work in August. Good grief.

"Congratulations."

"Thanks."

They didn't say anything else until Bell had consumed half his mug, at which point the caffeine kicked in and the world outside of Chris started to come into focus.

Bell blinked at the huge, gleaming armoire standing to the left of the hall that led to the back of the shop. It looked familiar. It had to be the same piece Chris had been working on for weeks. Now that it was finally done and stained, Bell could picture it in a grand entry hall at some Victorian mansion, or—well, okay, he didn't know how to identify which period it belonged in, but it looked historical and solid and expensive as hell. A little white tag affixed to one of the brass knobs on the front read Sold in crimson Sharpie.

"You finished it."

"Had Chloe put the last coat on yesterday," Chris said proudly. "What do you think?"

"It's gorgeous." Bell barely resisted the urge to reach out and run his fingers over the smoothly sanded finish. He didn't want to leave fingerprints. "Nice attention to detail."

Chris smiled. "Thanks. It's the first really elaborate custom order I've done, so I'm glad it turned out."

"You said it's going to—" Bell racked his brain. "A hunting lodge or something, right? Mount Kelley?"

Nodding, Chris led the way back to the workshop, probably to spare Bell from being gawked at in his pj's. "Yeah, exactly. I'm supposed to deliver it Saturday." He sat on his rolling stool, slid away from Bell for a moment, and then planted his feet. "I know we usually try to spend some time together on Saturdays.... I don't suppose you want to tag along? I could use another set of hands."

Bell felt his pulse speed up a little at the suggestion, which was the first time he'd ever felt that way about a several-hours-long car trip to haul furniture. Of course every other time had been to help friends move, and with Chris it was more like a date—a date in a pickup truck to deliver an armoire. If Chris hadn't been standing right in front of him, Bell probably would have covered his face with his hands out of embarrassment. He was getting sappy about a trip to deliver furniture.

"Bell?" Chris asked, maybe not for the first time. Bell realized he'd been standing there like an idiot.

"Yes? I mean, yes! That sounds like a lot of fun."

Chris raised an eyebrow, obviously suspicious of Bell's enthusiasm.

"What? Mount Kelley is supposed to be really pretty, so it would be cool to see. Besides, I get to spend the day with my favorite woodworker." Bell leaned in to peck Chris on the cheek.

"It's a date, then," Chris said. "Fair warning, though. It's a good idea to bring a backpack with a change of clothes. It should be a single-day trip, but between what can go wrong with a delivery and the roads up there, if the weather goes bad, it's always good to be prepared just in case."

"It would be a shame if we got stuck in the middle of nowhere and had to snuggle up for warmth," Bell said, not at all convincingly. He smiled. "Don't worry, I'll be prepared for anything."

Judging from the cute flush creeping up Chris's cheeks, he knew exactly what Bell was getting at. "Um… good?"

"It will be," Bell assured him with a wink. Then he finished his coffee and pressed a quick kiss to Chris's cheek. "Okay, I'm going to go shower. Thanks for the coffee. And the invite. I hope you still like me after—how long is the car ride?"

Chris shrugged minutely and ducked his head a little. "Not long enough that I'm worried."

God, he was sweet.

Of course, then he ruined it by adding, "If you get too chatty, I'll just stick you in the back."

"Hilarious," Bell said, but he helped himself to another kiss anyway. "Okay. I really am going to shower now. Do some work or something, you slacker."

BELL DIDN'T see a lot of Chris between Monday and Saturday morning. It seemed like Chris was working even more than usual since he'd be away most of the weekend, and Bell had two calls from other local small businesses looking to drum up more interest.

150

Between those jobs and delivering pizza, he decided he'd better not schedule their consultation appointments until after Thanksgiving, to give himself time to research and brainstorm.

In the meantime Bell looked forward to spending quality time with Chris. They managed a few breakfast dates in the shop, and on Friday Bell convinced Chris to take an extended lunch break and make out with him upstairs for half an hour. But they never got past kissing, and Bell was getting hot under the collar again.

Okay, well past "getting." What would it take to convince Chris he didn't need an engraved invitation to touch Bell's dick? Chris had definitely enjoyed himself last time. Bell felt confident of that.

He resolutely packed a new bottle of lube and an unopened box of condoms in his overnight bag and tried not to think of the knowing look on Betty's face when he's checked out at the store. That was one aspect of small-town life he could do without.

When Bell came down the stairs early Saturday morning, Chris was in the showroom, wrapping a thick, quilted moving blanket around the armoire.

Which led Bell to an important question he hadn't considered before. "Uh, how are we getting that in the truck?"

"We're not," Chris assured him, cinching a strap around the quilt to keep it in place. Oh good. "We're putting it in the trailer."

Bell resisted the urge to whimper. "You have seen my noodle arms, right?"

Chris snorted and secured another strap. "Your muscle tone is fine. And I took out all the interior drawers and removed the doors. They're already wrapped. We just have to get this on the dolly."

Bell relaxed a little. "Okay, that sounds more reasonable."

It took some effort and a fair amount of maneuvering, but they got the trailer loaded and the pieces of the armoire secured so they wouldn't shift during the drive. Then Chris and Bell shoved their backpacks behind the seats in the truck. Chris hopped in the driver's seat, and Bell directed him in backing up until the trailer hitch lined up. Not that he needed much help. He'd obviously done it before.

There was nothing left to do but get in.

Chris had a classic rock station playing just loud enough to enjoy without interrupting conversation. Bell absently hummed along as Chris pulled out of the lot and pointed the truck toward the highway.

And then Bell remembered. He cleared his throat, turned in his seat so he could rummage through the side pockets of his backpack, and came up with the car charger for his cell phone.

Chris raised his eyebrows. "Am I boring you already?"

"Nope," Bell said placidly, setting his phone in the cup holder. He didn't need it yet.

"Then…?"

"You promised to deliver the armoire today, right?"

"Yes." Chris signaled and changed lanes, about to take the truck onto the on-ramp.

Bell cleared his throat again, mostly as an excuse to bring his hand up to his face to hide his smile. "Well, Mount Kelley is that way."

Chris turned his signal off. "Oh God. I knew that."

"Uh-huh." Bell patted his phone. "GPS."

"You remembered about the direction thing, huh?"

"I am very invested in having a nice weekend with you." Bell debated broaching the subject, especially so early. If the conversation went poorly, they'd have many hours of awkward silence to sit through, but…. "I feel like we don't get to spend a lot of quality time together, you know?" There. That didn't sound confrontational, right?

For a few interminable seconds, Chris didn't say anything. Bell chanced a glance at him out of the corner of his eye, but his expression remained inscrutable, and he kept his eyes on the road. Finally he said, in what seemed to Bell a needlessly careful tone, "You do?"

Bell tried to work out if he was kidding or offended or just oblivious. "I mean, I see you all the time, but you're always working." Oops. That definitely sounded accusatory and unsatisfied. Well, it was too late now. He might as well keep going. "I… I'm trying to figure you out, I guess. Do you need more space? Do you want to slow down?" It didn't seem like it, not with Chris suggesting they take a trip together, but Bell couldn't help the nagging insecurity when Chris didn't talk to him. They hadn't been intimate since that first time on Chris's couch, and that had mostly happened by accident.

"No," Chris said quickly. "No. That's not it at all. I just…." He huffed a sigh and merged as his lane ended. "It sounds so stupid, but I was worried you'd get sick of me."

What.

"You're right," Bell said after a heartbeat. "That does sound stupid." At Chris's stricken expression, Bell jumped to say, "Not that it's not, you know, a valid way to feel, I guess? But um… you don't have to worry with me. Hanging out with you is awesome. I *want* to do it all the time."

With someone else he might have worried he'd tipped his hand too soon. With Chris he mostly just thought about the few terrible things Chris had admitted about his previous relationship, and wondered how many ugly secrets he was going to have to speculate about until Chris finally opened up.

"I know you're busy," he said when Chris didn't respond. "You've got the shop and fixing up the house and stuff—"

"I'm busy because I wanted to be," Chris admitted. He glanced over at Bell, shame and apology written in the downturn of his mouth. "I've been putting off subcontracting some work, both at the shop and for the renovations on the house, because when I don't have anything to do, it's harder to forget that I'm…."

Alone. "You're not, though. Or you don't have to be, even on nights when I'm working. I've done the work-all-the-time thing. It's not good for you, even if you do enjoy it. Go play soccer with Will, or come up to my sweet apartment and we can sexile Lady Frances."

Chris laughed a little, though it still sounded strained. "Sure, we can do that."

He didn't *sound* sure, but maybe now wasn't the right time to press further. They still had a lot of driving ahead of them, and changing the subject would give Bell's subconscious time to work out a theory regarding Chris's possible sex hang-up. "Good," Bell said cheerfully. "So what are your feelings on road-trip snacks?"

"DID YOU decide what you want to do for Thanksgiving?" Chris asked a few hours later, after successfully navigating from one highway to another.

Bell blew out a long breath. "I don't want to go home. Even if I could get the time off, it's just too much, between travel and fending off the Inquisition."

That hung in the truck for a moment. Before Bell could ask if Chris's offer to hang out at Will and Kristine's still stood, Chris said, "I have a suggestion?"

"Shoot."

"Come with me to Will and Kristine's." They had talked about it, so Bell didn't know why Chris sounded so apprehensive or why his knuckles seemed almost too white on the wheel. "We'll have dinner, bow out early, and then spend the whole weekend together—no work, no renovations. I promise. Just… us."

Bell's cheeks warmed with pleasure and the insinuation that they could spend at least some of that alone time naked. "Yeah?"

"I wasn't exactly planning on having a Black Friday sale. All the shoppers in Pineville will be in the city." Chris lifted one shoulder. His ears had gone pink. "We don't have to—"

"It sounds perfect," Bell interrupted. "Really. Me, you, my apartment, your house—it sounds perfect. But are you sure you won't be bored?"

Chris coughed and smoothed a hand over his hair. "I'm sure we'll find something to do."

Fucking right they would. Without looking, Bell reached out and set his hand on Chris's thigh. He grinned as he leaned his head against the window to watch the billboard ads go by. *Jesus Saves!* and

Bob Evans 3 Miles bracketed a giant picture of an eggplant that read *Grade A Substitutes. Purple Passion Adult Toys.*

Maybe Bell should take notes of all the highway sex shops they could do business with.

Better yet, maybe he could convince Chris they should visit in person.

They passed signs for an antique shop, an advertisement for romantic mountain cottage rentals, and a billboard shilling for a divorce lawyer who specialized in securing custody for male parents. Then it almost became a pattern: restaurant (*Family style!*), shopping center (*Over 100 stores*), online college (*Learning at your fingertips. Degrees at your pace*), restaurant (*Best sushi out of town!*), sex shop (*Explore your wild side*), lawyer (*Because you deserve better*).

Chris's hand covered Bell's, and he smiled with his eyes half-closed. He always got sleepy in the car when he didn't have to drive.

Restaurant, college, legal aid for abused women, donate your car to charity, sex shop.

His eyelids drifted closed.

Then they hit a pothole and Bell's eyes snapped open.

Oh. Shit.

"Hey," he said as neutrally as he could, "can I ask you something?"

"Hmm," Chris answered. Bell took that as a yes.

"It's about DJ," he warned.

"I'll try not to drive off the road."

That was probably as much as Bell could hope for. He took a deep breath. Now he just had to figure out the least offensive way to phrase his question.

Fuck it.

"Was he as much of an asshole in bed as he is out of it?"

He tried not to hold his breath and waited to see if he'd mortally offended his boyfriend.

Chris seemed to be holding his breath too, or maybe Bell's question had turned him to stone. But finally the strains of "Gimme Shelter" faded out, and Chris said, "That depends on what you mean by asshole, I guess."

Bell decided that qualified as another yes. "Jesus."

"It wasn't like that," Chris protested. Bell didn't know what that meant. "He didn't do anything illegal."

Christ, Bell hadn't even considered that. His stomach flipped. He wished he'd tried harder to be tactful. "Jesus," he repeated. "None of this is lessening my desire to punch him in his stupid face."

Was he going to have to ask what DJ did?

He was trying to decide if that was something he could do or whether Chris would rather he back off when Chris said, "It's just that he never let me forget that I'm not very...."

Bell waited, tasting bile.

"Good at it," Chris finished quietly and continued to stare at the road.

Bell saw red.

"Take the next exit," he said tersely.

That made Chris look over. "What?"

"Find a hotel," Bell told him. "Or a motel. Hell, find a parking lot with convenient tree cover."

"We're forty-five minutes from the lodge, according to your GPS. Why?"

"Because DJ isn't here for me to punch right now, and the next best thing is proving him wrong in absentia." Bell paused and then frowned. "No, wait. I take that back. Proving him wrong is inherently better, because I also get to have awesome sex with you."

Chris squirmed. "You don't have to lie to make me feel better. I'd rather you were honest with me."

Bell's hands curled into fists. He pressed them into his thighs and tried to let the pain ground him, to give his rage an outlet. "You want honesty? I hate that this asshole treated you like shit. I hate that he made you second-guess yourself. I hate that you've been keeping me at arm's length because he made you feel like you

156

weren't worth knowing. And on a slightly more frivolous note, I hate that I could have been having the best sex of my life for the past few weeks, but I haven't, and it turns out that's also your ex's fault."

Oops. The rage found an outlet, all right.

For a few seconds, Chris fishmouthed. Then he asked, hesitantly, "The best sex of your life?"

He sounded like he believed it. Or at least like he wanted to. Thank God.

"Find a motel," Bell repeated seriously.

Chris sped up.

BELL ALMOST tripped over his backpack as they crashed through the door to their room, attached at the mouth and the hips. Initially he was going to drop the bag. By the time he remembered that he'd packed optimistically and he was going to want immediate access to its contents, he'd accidentally put his foot through the shoulder strap.

Chris caught him before he could fall, and both of them laugh-panted breathlessly into each other's mouths as they hit the bed with a squeak of springs. Bell winced as his phone dug into his thigh. He squirmed until he could remove it from his pocket and then threw it toward the nightstand, grabbed two fistfuls of Chris's shirt, and reeled him in for another kiss.

But as good as it felt—the bristly tickle of Chris's beard on his skin, the softness of his lips, the steady pressure of his tongue against Bell's—none of it satisfied Bell for long. He worked one of his feet onto the bed and used the leverage to push Chris onto his back.

Chris let out a surprised breath as he hit the hard mattress, but he recovered quickly enough to steady Bell as he straddled his waist, reaching for the buttons of Chris's shirt. "I should take all your clothes off this time," Bell said, hungrily eyeing each centimeter of skin he revealed.

"Okay," Chris said half a beat later, amused but a little too soft. Self-conscious, but Bell could get Chris past that. He finished with the buttons and leaned down to suck a soft kiss onto the skin of Chris's collarbone, but the heat of Chris's skin was addictive. As he pushed the fabric past Chris's shoulders, he moved his mouth down the center of Chris's chest and then bit lightly just to the right of his belly button.

Chris snorted a laugh, and Bell hid his smile against Chris's stomach. "Troublemaker," Chris accused, obviously fond.

Bell bit him again, a little lower this time, and held eye contact as he did it. Then he thumbed open the button of Chris's fly and eased the zipper down.

In Bell's estimation, Chris had no reason to feel self-conscious. Maybe his body didn't look like it'd been photoshopped, but neither did Bell's.

He paused long enough to pull his shirt off and went back to working Chris's jeans down his thighs. Chris's erection had already pushed through the gap of his fly and strained at the front of his boxer briefs. Bell licked his lips. He wanted it in his mouth again, but— maybe in round two.

He'd just gotten Chris's jeans to his knees when the bed started to vibrate. Bell wondered if they managed to get a motel bed that had Magic Fingers, but then he saw that his phone hadn't quite made it to the table and was buzzing beside Chris's head.

God, it was probably his mother. "We're ignoring that," he said firmly and got Chris's jeans the rest of the way off. His socks came with them, which was fortunate; there was no sexy way to take off someone's socks.

"No argument from me," Chris said. As the phone went silent, he reached for Bell. "Now either take your pants off or come here and let me do it."

"Not that I don't appreciate the offer, but in the interests of getting naked as fast as possible...." Bell stood, gracelessly shoved his jeans down, and crawled back onto the bed and into Chris's arms.

"Hi," Chris said when they were nose-to-nose.

Bell grinned. "Hi."

The phone rang again, and he giggled in spite of himself as he leaned down to claim Chris's mouth. He felt a bit like a teenager missing curfew. Chris ran his hands down Bell's back, and Bell shivered pleasantly in encouragement and groaned when Chris cupped his bare ass. He couldn't resist, so he rolled his hips and rubbed his dick against Chris's through the fabric of Chris's underwear, even though his backpack with the lube in it was a foot and a half from his hand. He didn't want to rush.

Okay, he wanted to rush a little.

The buzzing cut off, and Bell reached over the side of the bed, resting some of his weight on Chris so he could fish in the front pocket for the bottle. He closed his fingers around it—

And the phone rang.

This time Bell paused, poised awkwardly on one arm, and met Chris's eyes.

"Do you want to answer it?" Chris asked with a slight grimace.

Bell groaned and dropped his head to Chris's shoulder. "No." But chances were, if someone had called three times in a row, it was important. Or they thought so, anyway. At the very least, he should check. "Don't go anywhere," he said into Chris's bicep, and then he reached for the phone.

One missed call from his sister and two from his mother, who was calling again. If they wanted to give him career advice, he was going to block their numbers until after New Year's. He shifted to one side and sat cross-legged on the mattress beside Chris. He knew he must look ridiculous, but he accepted the call and tried not to sound irritated. "Hello?"

"Oh thank God, Bell," said the caller, all in a rush. Bell frowned. That wasn't his mother's voice.

"Emily? Why are you calling from Mom's phone?"

"My battery died. I've been calling and calling. You have to come home."

Bell wanted to protest. He already had plans; his mother was a pain in the ass; his family made him feel like a black sheep. But Emily had always been composed, and now she sounded near tears. "I'm on a weekend road trip in the other direction. What's going on?"

"It's Cam," she said. "He had a heart attack."

CHAPTER TWELVE

BELL WAS vaguely aware of Emily talking about which hospital he needed to get to and how Monica was doing and what the doctor said about Cam's condition. But he couldn't concentrate on any of it. He couldn't make it stick. Finally someone took the phone from his hand and spoke to Emily in quiet but composed tones. Eventually the call ended, the phone was placed on the bureau, and Chris pulled Bell into his arms.

Bell knew he should say something, but his mind was a jumble. Chris patted his hair for a while and then said, "You know, we have our overnight bags. I can have Chloe or Will watch Lady Frances and you can call into work for a few days. There's an airport twenty minutes from the lodge.. So you give the word and we'll be on our way."

Bell's hand found Chris's unoccupied one, and their fingers laced together. "All right," he said as he finally recovered his voice. "Take me home."

IT WASN'T until they stood outside hospital room 237 God knew how many travel hours later that Bell's brain came back online. It immediately began working overtime. "Oh my God."

Chris looked at him, glanced briefly at their linked hands, and asked, "What?"

"I didn't even ask if you wanted to come." Now that the shock of Cam's heart attack and the mind-numbing fuzz of travel had worn off, several facts hit him at once. He was about to introduce Chris to his family—his family, who didn't even know he had a boyfriend, because he hadn't told them, and who hadn't been introduced to any of Bell's boyfriends since he dated that asshole his first year of college. And

Chris didn't realize that Bell's family would be dicks about it. Jesus. Everyone was going into this situation blind because Bell couldn't stick up for himself and his choices. "Can you even take time off?"

Chris made as if to let go of Bell's hand. "Do you not want me here?"

Bell didn't let him. "Of course I want you here, but that doesn't mean I get to be selfish about it."

"That's exactly what it means." Chris squeezed his fingers. "Now break it down for me. What's on the other side of this door?"

In an attempt to calm himself, Bell reached for his humor and a deep breath. "Well, not, like, *literal* danger or anything, but you might prefer that to my actual family."

"You're worth the risk," Chris said, and he opened the door.

Bell blinked for a moment when they stepped inside. The room was smaller than he expected, and Mom, Emily, and Monica were crowded around a bed so small that Cam seemed to fill it up. At the same time, though, he looked pale and insignificant propped up against the pillows. Bell was used to seeing him looking tan and fit in Armani suits, not sallow and stubbled in a pale blue hospital gown. For the first time, Bell could see how Cam resembled Grandpa Walt. He swallowed hard and tried not to think about that.

"Hey, bro," Bell said lamely. He tried to think of something upbeat or even funny, but nothing would come.

Then Chris moved so that his shoulder, warm and solid, brushed against Bell's. He leaned into it a bit, which must have caught Cam's attention, because Cam said, in a voice that wanted to seem strong but lacked a lot of its usual energy, "Who's your friend?"

"Wow, can't get one past you." Bell grinned at him anemically, grateful for a conversation starter. "This is Chris McGregor. Chris, this is Mom and Emily and Cameron and Monica. Everyone, this is my, um… boyfriend, Chris, who I promise I wasn't intending to introduce to you like this."

Cam shot Bell a look that seemed to say, "Oh yeah, so when were you?" but he just waved with the hand that didn't have tubes and tape all over it.

Chris nodded and said hello, and everyone else murmured a "Hi. Nice to meet you." It was awkward as hell.

Fortunately Chris seemed to know how to handle it, because he said, "I noticed the little cafe when we came in. We had kind of a rough flight, and I could use a coffee. Can I get anyone else anything?"

Bell's family came to the general consensus of "Yes, please," so much so that Emily volunteered to be Chris's extra set of hands. At least they'd spoken on the phone, so Bell wasn't actually throwing Chris to the wolves. In fact, all the wolves were staying in the room with him.

Maybe he should've volunteered to go too, but he just got there, and Cam was his brother.

"So," Bell said. He tried not to squirm as Chris and Emily's footsteps faded down the hallway. "You got so upset that I wasn't coming home for Thanksgiving you had to have a heart attack?"

He still couldn't believe it. Not really. His older brother had always seemed invincible.

"Bellamy," his mother chastened, swatting at him, but he'd made her smile, even if only weakly.

Cam laughed a little, but no color came to his cheeks. "Not that I'm not happy to see you, but the doc is blaming this one on stress-induced high blood pressure and not enough sleep."

Oh God. Bell's whole family was doomed to die young. "Yeah, you really should be stockpiling z's for when the next little one arrives."

"Looks like I'll have no choice now. Doctor's orders." Cam gave Monica a soft look. They were holding hands. Bell saw the reassuring squeeze, though he wasn't sure who was reassuring whom. "But seriously. I got pretty lucky. Mild heart attacks still suck, though."

"I can imagine," Bell said, trying for levity. "You look like hell."

"Bellamy!" his mother scolded again. "Be nice to your brother. He's in the hospital."

Funny. Bell hadn't noticed.

"I hope you didn't have to cancel anything important to come," Cam said. "Really, it's not that big of a deal. You didn't have to take off work."

Rolling his eyes, Bell picked his way to Emily's vacated chair and claimed it for himself and his tired ass. He slumped in the chair and dry scrubbed his face. How long had he been awake? What time was it, even? Or what day? "I'm sure Pineville can manage without pizza delivery for a few days."

The room went oddly silent. Bell blinked and tried to identify what he'd said that made everything stop.

"Pizza delivery?" his mother echoed, sounding confused.

And oh. Bell hadn't meant to open that can of worms, but the lies had been exhausting him for weeks. Apparently he was literally too tired to lie to his mother. "Yeah. Pizza delivery," he said, injecting the words with as much backbone as he could muster. "I'm trying something new."

In his peripheral vision, he saw Monica and Cam exchange glances.

"I'm just going to use the facilities," Monica said quietly. Bell might have tried to help her up if he'd been less tired. But she heaved herself to her feet and waddled—not because she was huge yet but, Bell assumed, because she had to pee—at a surprisingly quick rate to the en suite bathroom.

Bell watched Cam watch her go. Cam looked betrayed.

Then their mother rounded on Bell, and it was time to pay attention. Her eyes flashed as she narrowed them. "You told me you were doing freelance consulting work."

Bell had a few options. He could tell the absolute truth. But it shouldn't matter *what* he decided to do with his life as long as he was happy. And even the idea of having the conversation here, in his brother's hospital room... it just struck him as trivial, under the circumstances. "Is that really important right now?"

His mother made a pinched face. "You didn't tell me you had a boyfriend. You didn't tell me you were working as a delivery boy. I don't understand why you've been lying to me!"

"Because if I don't, I'm going to end up like *that*!" Bell exploded, pointing at his brother.

You could have heard a pin drop.

His mother looked like she'd been slapped.

Fuck. There was no taking it back now. He could only go forward and hope she'd finally understand. "Mom, I love you, but I can't do it. Okay? I hated that office job. I never saw the sun. I worked so much I rarely even saw my bed. You know why I quit? I was working late with my boss. It was like two in the morning. I went home at three the day before. But we were working a deadline, and it had to get done. So I went to the all-night coffee shop across the street to get the biggest cups I could, even though my stomach felt so gross I hadn't been able to eat anything but white rice and bananas all week." His mother flinched. "I got there and the barista was singing along to the radio, sweeping the floor and using the broom handle as a microphone. And I would've given anything to trade her places. We finished the project, and I quit."

She took a breath. "Not every job—"

So she hadn't gotten the point. "You want to know why I lied? Because nothing is ever good enough for you unless you have the biggest house, the shiniest car, the corner office, the best promotion. The fattest bonus. But that stuff didn't make me happy, Mom. It was killing me. So I picked my happiness over making you proud."

Now she looked like she was going to cry. Meanwhile in the bed, poor Cam was probably frantically stabbing the morphine button, since he was stuck witnessing a train wreck. Did they give morphine to heart attack patients?

"Oh honey." Bell's mom touched her perfectly lipsticked mouth and did something Bell had never seen her do: she wiped her eye with the back of one hand and smeared her mascara. She actually sniffed instead of taking a Kleenex from her purse and dabbing delicately at her nose. "I'm sorry. I only wanted to make sure you had the tools to be happy and financially secure."

"I don't need to make six figures to have a good life, Mom. I'm a delivery guy right now because I needed a break and it pays the bills. But what if that made me happy? Could you live with that? Instead of pushing me to do something else?"

"I'll try," she promised. "I might need you to remind me sometimes, but I'll try."

Bell exhaled, expelling a knot of tension that had been growing since who knew when. But he wasn't done. "And can you apply the same logic to my boyfriend? Because"—*I love him*—"he's the best thing in my life right now, and I'll be really upset if you make him feel like he's not good enough."

"Baby. You're really happy?" She took a step forward and reached for his hands. For once he truly believed that nothing else mattered to her.

He let her take his hands and squeezed. "Yeah, Mom. I really am."

"Oh thank God. Coffee," Cam said loudly from the bed, and Bell startled and looked up. Chris and Emily stood in the doorway.

"*You* can have juice," their mother said firmly, turning away from Bell. "The doctor hasn't cleared you for caffeine."

"That's fine," Cam said easily. "I won't need it when I quit my job to become a bartender at a tiki lounge. Monica! You can come out now. Mom didn't cry and Bell didn't explode."

Bell wanted to roll his eyes at his brother's theatrics, but he caught Chris's gaze over his mother's shoulder and wondered how much Chris had overheard. At least a little, if the soft flush to his cheeks were any gauge, but neither he nor Emily said anything about it.

"Yes. We brought coffee," Chris said, walking into the room with a tray balanced in his hands. "I make no promises about drinkability, though."

"I've had my share of hospital coffee in my day," Bell's mom said. She smiled as she picked up a paper cup. "Lord knows I spent enough time waiting for Bell's father to finish his shift so I could drive him home. I'm Liz." Wow, the short name, even. She was really pulling out all the stops. "And I think Bell introduced you as Chris?"

166

Chris flashed a quick glance at Bell and set the tray down. "Yes, ma'am. Chris McGregor." He held out his hand.

Bell's mom took him by the shoulders and looked into his eyes. "Never call me ma'am again," she said seriously. Chris looked like he wanted to run away, but Bell's mom pulled him into a hug before he could. "Thank you for taking care of my son."

Bell had officially entered the twilight zone.

"He's no trouble, mostly," Chris said, half-awkward and half-teasing, as he submitted to the hug. When Bell's mother let him go, he plucked a cup off the tray and offered it to Bell. "This one's yours. Decaf."

Probably a good idea. Bell didn't know exactly how long he'd been awake, but his eyelids felt like sandpaper. "Thanks."

They stuck around for an hour or so, until Bell felt reassured his brother wasn't going to slip away in the night. But around Bell's twelve hundredth yawn, Chris asked, "Is there a hotel nearby? We haven't slept in, uh." He squinted at the clock. Bell wondered where his glasses were. "However long it's been. We could use a break and a shower."

"Oh, don't be ridiculous, dear." Bell's mother reached into her purse and withdrew the keys to her Jag. "You can stay with us. We have plenty of room, and Bell knows where everything is. Emily can give me a ride home later."

Bell stared blankly at the keys in Chris's hand. "You sure?"

His mom waved him off. "Let me just call your father and find out if Mandy's sleeping."

Bell had just enough energy to direct Chris to his parents' house, though he fought yawns most of the way. When they got there, his dad was passed out on the sofa with Mandy in the playpen in front of him. Fortunately she was also asleep.

"You can meet them later," Bell said around a yawn and pulled Chris upstairs by the wrist. "Come on."

Bell's bedroom hadn't been Bell's bedroom in years, but his mother believed in keeping up appearances, so she had the housekeeper change the sheets every two weeks. Bell dropped his backpack by the foot of the bed and waited while Chris did the same. Then he blinked blearily at the small en suite bath. "I should shower."

Chris snorted. "You'll drown," he said. "Come on. Take your clothes off and I'll get you a facecloth, okay?"

That sounded a lot more manageable than a shower. Bell undressed and sat on the edge of the bed to run the warm cloth over his face. Then he let Chris nudge him over in the bed and climb in after him. "Was that a train wreck?" he muttered into Chris's shoulder.

"Maybe just a small one," Chris said teasingly, and Bell smiled in spite of himself.

"I guess I can live with that. 'M gonna pass out now."

"'Kay."

Bell was asleep before he could say anything else.

HE WOKE up in what he assumed was the middle of the night to the mattress dipping beside him. "Mmm?" he asked.

"I woke up and smelled myself and couldn't get back to sleep," Chris answered, sounding sheepish, and Bell pried his eyes open as a smile tugged at his lips. He could only just see Chris's silhouette as the moonlight seeped through the blinds, but his hair glistened with moisture.

Bell opened his mouth and searched for an appropriate affectionate taunt, but when he inhaled, he caught a whiff of himself and shoved at Chris instead. "God. Move over and let me out. I reek."

Chris let out a soft snort, traded places with him, and snuggled into the warm space left by Bell's body as Bell stumbled toward the bathroom. Bell wanted to crawl back into bed... but no. Ugh. He had airport *and* hospital all over him. Gross.

He didn't hurry, because the last thing he wanted was to come back smelling less than fresh, but he didn't dawdle either. He dried off as fast as he could, gave his wet hair a few scrubs with a fluffy towel, and reached for his clean sleep clothes—which weren't there. He'd been so grossed out that he hadn't bothered to go through his bag to grab anything to put on. Bell looked at his boxers and tee, crumpled in a pile on the floor. There was no way he was putting those back on. He hung up his towel and quietly slipped back into the bedroom. The soft, deep, slightly wheezy breaths told him that Chris was out like a light, but he couldn't be disappointed as he slipped between the sheets next to him.

They'd had a long day, and Bell couldn't have asked for Chris to handle his family and the entire situation any better than he had. Bell was very grateful, and if he had to wait until morning to show it, that was just fine. He rolled over so he was nearly nestled against Chris's shoulder and could breathe in the scent of him and bask in the warmth. As soon as he registered just how content he was, Bell fell fast asleep.

WHEN BELL next woke up, he was very warm, and Chris had snuggled up behind him. Bell stayed still for a moment and tried not to wake him, but the nuzzling at the back of his neck was definitely conscious. So was the hard-on he could feel against his ass, though Bell guessed Chris was trying not to be conspicuous about it.

That wouldn't do at all.

Bell rocked his hips back just enough to let Chris know he was awake and that Chris definitely didn't need to be shy.

"Good morning," Chris murmured into the crook of his neck. "Sleep well?"

"Woke up better," Bell answered as he tugged Chris's hand over to rest on his abdomen.

"I didn't mean to wake you up."

"Believe me," Bell said, voice hitching a bit as Chris took some initiative and smoothed his hand lower, "I don't mind."

"So I see," he said, trailing his nose over the shell of Bell's ear. Then he paused with his nails scratching lightly through the hair below Bell's navel. "Did you forget something after your shower?"

Bell tilted his head back, hoping Chris would take the hint. He did, and his soft lips were a perfect contrast to the scratch of his beard. "Maybe I was thinking ahead."

Chris nipped the skin over Bell's pulse and moved his hand down farther to tease around the base of Bell's cock. "You want to pick up where we left off?" Bell felt acutely aware of the sticky press of Chris's cock between his cheeks.

"Yes, please." No point being shy about what he wanted. He flailed blindly next to the bed and came up with the strap of his backpack, which he pulled onto the bed. Chris drew a single finger lightly up the length of Bell's erection as Bell scrambled in the side pocket for the lube. Thank God the TSA was getting more lenient.

Finally he closed his hand around the tube and a strip of foil packets. He shoved the backpack off the bed and dropped the condoms beside his pillow so he wouldn't lose them. Then he flicked open the cap of the lube and reached down to grab Chris's wrist. "Give me your hand."

Chris opened his hand so Bell could drizzle the lube over his fingers. By the time Chris gripped Bell's cock, Bell was very eager. He rocked forward into Chris's hand. Chris stroked him just a bit harder than a tease, rubbing over the head with his thumb slowly enough that it felt like Chris wanted to jerk him off all morning. Eager as he was, it suited Bell to have a somewhat sleepy pace now that they weren't caught up in the heat of the moment. He felt like they'd been on the verge forever, and he wanted it to be good for Chris.

Chris ground himself against Bell's ass. It didn't feel like Bell had anything to worry about. Bell pressed back to give Chris a little more friction and a clear invitation. He let Chris hear him a little too, and he was even more thankful now that his younger self had insisted on the bedroom upstairs and on the other side of the house from the master suite.

The moving and the moaning did the trick, because Chris slid his hand lower, to the base of Bell's cock and then to his balls, and cupped and rolled them gently in his hand.

"Yeah," Bell breathed and tried to shift so Chris would have a better avenue to move where Bell wanted him to touch most. When Chris pressed his fingers just behind his balls, Bell let out a moan that couldn't be mistaken for anything but encouragement. He hoped Chris didn't mind that Bell sounded a little bit slutty when he got going. When Chris's fingertips caught the edge of Bell's rim, Chris made a hungry sound and sucked hard at the side of Bell's throat. The angle was about to get difficult, but Bell couldn't resist tilting his hips in an effort to get more.

Chris made that noise again and set his teeth against the sensitive skin of Bell's neck, just over what Bell could already tell would be a red-purple bruise. But as Bell half choked on how much he wanted to feel Chris's fingers inside him, Chris sighed in apparent frustration and moved his hand to Bell's thigh instead, coaxing him to draw his knee up toward his chest. "Need longer arms for that," he said apologetically while Bell was still feeling the rush of heat from being made so blatantly accessible.

"I," he started, but any witty retort he might have come up with died on his lips when Chris slid his hand between Bell's cheeks and let his fingertips flirt with Bell's hole. Bell exhaled heavily, feeling as taut as a bowstring as Chris played him. "Oh." His voice sounded high and strained.

He needed more.

"Chris, come on. I—" Chris rubbed his fingers in a slick, firm circle. "I've been waiting," Bell said plaintively. Hadn't he been patient for weeks and weeks? That patience had run out.

"Wait a little longer," Chris said, his voice hoarse. "It'll be worth it." And then he finally pressed one finger inside.

The slide of it and the sudden pressure made Bell's eyes roll back. He held his breath and cataloged everything—Chris's mouth on his shoulder, his tongue licking idly, the scratch of his beard, the touch of Chris's finger inside him and on his cheeks, their scents mingled together on the sheets. "Yes," Bell said. He wanted to arch into the touch, but with his leg pulled up, he didn't have any leverage.

It didn't matter. Chris knew what he needed. And maybe he was impatient too, because he'd only fucked his finger in a handful of times—Bell's heart stopped and started again with each thrust—when he pushed a second finger in beside it.

Bell tried to rock back to make Chris go deeper or faster, or both. But Chris was determined to use up every last bit of Bell's patience, because he didn't do either. He worked his slick fingers in slowly and more shallowly than Bell really needed, at an angle that was just shy of making Bell crazy for it.

"Come on," Bell almost whined, not that it made any difference. Chris just fingerfucked him as though he had all day to make Bell come and was in no hurry at all to get his dick into him. That made one of them.

"Chris…." He trailed off in a hiss as Chris crooked his fingers just right and made Bell buck his hips and clench around them. Chris swore under his breath and then nipped at Bell's shoulder.

"You like that," he said and did it again.

"Yeah," Bell said. He meant "Yes. Please. That's so good. More of that," or "Just go ahead and fuck me already," but he was reduced to single syllables. Chris was going to wreck him slowly and thoroughly and gather him back up again afterward. Bell sank the fingers of one hand into a pillow and reached back with the other to pat clumsily at Chris's hip.

Chris must have understood what he wanted, because he did it again and again and again, until Bell couldn't bite his lip to keep quiet anymore and his needy gasps escaped with every thrust and curl of Chris's fingers. When he stopped long enough to apply more lube, Bell thought he'd die waiting, but then Chris pushed inside him again, and suddenly Bell heard a crinkle of foil and the scent of latex hit his nose.

Soon. God, *soon*.

"Yes," he said again. He clenched and released and relished the shiver Chris's full-body shudder sent through him. Chris's warm, latex-smooth cock pressed against his asscheek. "I want you. *Now*, Chris. Don't make me wait. I can't—I can't wait any longer."

172

Chris rasped his beard up Bell's neck and shoulder to mouth at his ear, but he took him at his word. "Okay, shh," he said. He withdrew his fingers and set his slick hand on Bell's hip to position him as he pushed closer. "Let me just—"

Bell cried out as Chris pushed inside him. The movement was unhurried—just a slow, inevitable slide. Bell's skin felt too tight, as though it couldn't contain the pleasure building within him, waiting to snap. He pressed his head back against Chris's shoulder, but the angle strained his neck. It was awkward until Chris slipped an arm beneath him to compensate and support Bell's body. Then Bell could only squeeze his eyes shut and pant as his stomach muscles tightened.

Chris swore quietly against Bell's nape and then adjusted until his breath tickled Bell's ear. His mouth was hot around Bell's earlobe, and Bell's spine melted. "You feel amazing."

Bell made a strangled sound that he hoped Chris would interpret as agreement. He *did* feel amazing. Trapped against Chris's body, held captive by a hand on his hip and a cock in his ass and an arm around his chest, palm pressed to his heart, he knew he'd been right—best sex of his life. Too bad he couldn't articulate that, though the way he kept hitching his hips fruitlessly back and forth to get Chris to fuck him harder probably conveyed his enthusiasm.

Bell wasn't going to last.

"Fuck," he breathed and curled his fingers hard into the pillow. "Chris. Oh my God."

"Good?"

"Uuuuh," Bell answered. He wanted to reach for his dick, but he couldn't move. Chris had the perfect angle, and his cock rubbed Bell's prostate just right. "Can you...."

"This?" Chris guessed and moved his slick hand from Bell's hip to his erection.

Bell's breath came in short, ragged gasps as he fought orgasm. "Kiss me," he begged. He turned his head, but he couldn't quite turn far enough.

173

Chris's lips touched his, and all the tiny hairs on the back of Bell's neck stood up. But he still couldn't get the depth he wanted from the kiss, couldn't—

Chris raised his hand to Bell's cheek and helped him turn that fraction of an inch more. Bell opened his mouth into the kiss.

The second Chris's tongue brushed over his, he lost himself. Orgasm rushed through him—his hole clenched, his nipples tightened, the world washed out in a wave of white. Chris groaned against his lips and stroked him through pleasure that seemed to go on and on, until Bell had to break away from the kiss because he was still coming and couldn't get enough air. God. *God.*

Chris pressed his forehead to the back of Bell's neck and shook against him.

Holy fuck.

It would probably be inappropriate to say "I told you so."

Bell flailed blindly for Chris's hand. It was sticky, but so was everything at this point. He laced their fingers together for a squeeze.

Chris squeezed back and sweetly dropped a kiss at the edge of Bell's hairline. He seemed almost shy. Neither of them moved or spoke for a few heartbeats. Finally Bell caught his breath and his brain unfroze. As Chris softened and slipped out of him, Bell rolled cautiously to one side and realized the sheets were a lost cause anyway. *Fuck it.*

A lovely flush had spread across Chris's nose and cheeks, and his blue eyes burned brightly. The hint of a smile around his mouth held a note of wonder.

Definitely worth an "I told you so," but Bell would rather preserve the mood. He rubbed their noses together, and Chris bussed his lips for a kiss that lingered without deepening.

"We need another shower," Chris said ruefully when their mouths parted.

"Mmm," Bell agreed, pushing back the sheets. Oh yeah. He was definitely doing laundry today. Oops. Then he pulled Chris up out of bed with him. "Come on. I bet we'll both fit." He wasn't taking any chances. He suspected Chris needed more cuddles, shower comment notwithstanding. And even if he didn't, Bell doubted he'd object to fooling around in the bathroom.

He was right about that, though they didn't get beyond a few soap-slick gropes and shampoo-flavored kisses. After the weekend they'd had, Bell figured neither of them had much left in the tank. His suspicion was proven when Bell's stomach rumbled loudly as they were drying off.

"Anyone would think I don't feed you," Chris teased and swatted him over the towel.

"I promise I won't let anyone think that." Bell batted his eyelashes, then lifted a shoulder. "If you find me something to eat, I'll do the laundry."

Chris's ears went red. "I can't believe I did that in your parents' house."

"Me neither. Teenage me is fist-pumping right now."

Chris groaned and put his face in his hands.

Bell patted him on the shoulder. "Relax. I'm pretty sure my dad's back at the hospital by now. We probably have the place to ourselves. Think you can find the kitchen?"

"How big can this house be?" Chris said optimistically.

"That's the spirit."

Bell had never been so thankful that his mother insisted on a second-floor laundry. He stripped the bed, then dumped the sheets and, after a moment's consideration, their clothes from the day before, into the washing machine and started it.

He found Chris in the kitchen, staring intently at the french press as he slowly depressed the plunger. "Hey. You found coffee."

"Yes," Chris agreed. The back of his neck still seemed red. Maybe from the shower. Bell wanted to kiss it. "That's not all I found," he said meaningfully.

Uh-oh. "Dad's still around, huh?" Bell said, wincing. Well, on the plus side, after his mother, his father wasn't especially threatening.

"I'm probably lucky he isn't the 'shoot first, ask questions later' type."

"Oh God. I really thought he'd be back at the hospital."

"He had to wait for Monica's mom to pick up Mandy, and she was running late, apparently." Chris finished with the coffee and poured the first mug. "He did offer to fix my nose."

"He did not," Bell said. God, had his father gotten worse while he was away?

Chris's lips twitched. "He did." At least he didn't seem offended.

Bell groaned and went to the fridge for the creamer.

Ugh. He hoped they'd been quiet.

When the thought occurred to him, he jerked and smacked his head on the handle of the freezer in his haste to turn back around. "He didn't say anything about...."

If possible, Chris went redder. "Ah, no. He didn't."

Small mercies. Bell relaxed a bit and set the creamer on the counter. "Well, I'm still sorry. I haven't been very *present* for the whole meet-the-parents thing. You have my permission to throw me to the wolves when I meet yours."

Chris stared at him, his mouth slightly open and his eyes very warm. "What?"

Chris shook his head minutely and then cleared his throat. "When you meet my parents."

"Yeah?" Bell said. "It's bound to happen eventually, right?" A few more weeks and Christmas would be upon them. Surely it wasn't that much of a stretch—

"I love you," Chris said.

Oh.

Bell told himself to be cool, but he couldn't do anything to stop the smile spreading across his face or the heat rushing to his cheeks. "Yeah?" he repeated, then immediately felt stupid. His feet carried him forward, into the range of Chris's arms. Outside his family, no one had told him that before, and Bell had never said it either.

"Yeah," Chris said, tugging Bell closer by the waistband of his jeans. All things considered, he was pretty confident for a guy who'd just dropped the L-word into a relationship for the first time and hadn't heard it back. He must be pretty sure Bell was head over heels for him. Finally, Bell felt pretty smug about that.

He looped his arms around Chris's neck and grinned at him. Bell's voice only cracked a little when he said, "You love me back?"

Ah, there it was—a glimmer of the man with the crumbled self-esteem. Bell could feel it when the tension seeped out of Chris's shoulders. That shy smile held a dry edge, but Chris's eyes held nothing but sweetness. "Yeah. You want me to say it again?"

Was that a trick question? "Yeah," Bell said immediately, nodding. Their faces had grown very close together, and their noses bumped, but they never broke eye contact.

As soon as Chris opened his mouth, though, someone behind Bell cleared their throat.

Damn it.

"Good morning, Bell."

Well, it was. Bell refused to pull away from Chris before he got a kiss, even if he'd originally been angling for something else. Then he turned around. "Hi, Dad."

"Can I borrow you for a minute?"

Oh good, a talk his dad didn't want to have in front of his boyfriend. And the day had started off so well. Still, no reason to drag Chris down with him. "Sure," Bell said as neutrally as he could and pressed another quick kiss to Chris's cheek. "Check the freezer. Mom stockpiles Pillsbury for bad days."

Chris looked affronted at the suggestion of frozen pastry, so hopefully that would at least distract him from whatever family torment Bell was going to submit himself to next.

Bell followed his father into the living room. "What's up?"

His father took off his glasses, rubbed his nose, and then ran a hand through his salt-and-pepper hair. "Your mother told me what you said to her yesterday."

Bell's stomach went sour. He knew he'd gotten off too easily with his mother's reaction. She was going to force his dad to be the bad guy. "Okay. And?" He tried to keep his tone as even as possible. No need to invite more trouble than he had already.

177

"And it took a lot of guts to stand up to your mother like that." The glasses went back on. "I'm proud of you. And I'm sorry you haven't felt supported." He grimaced slightly. "No, I'm sorry we haven't *been* supportive. We're going to do better. I promise."

Bell blinked. It was too early in the morning—or maybe just too soon after orgasm—for his brain to have to go through so many emotions. "Thanks, Dad."

"No, thank *you*. I needed the reality check too." His dad smiled and then tilted his head to indicate the kitchen. "Now tell me about your new boyfriend."

Bell resisted the urge to look over his shoulder. He wouldn't be able to see Chris if he did anyway. The wall was in the way. "What do you want to know?"

"Let's start with the basics. Where he's from, what he does...." Bell's father cast him a significant look. "How old he is."

"He grew up in Pineville, moved around, moved back. He owns his own custom-carpentry business. He is none-of-your-business years old." His dad laughed at that, and Bell added spitefully, "And there's nothing wrong with his nose."

"Oh, so he doesn't snore?" his father asked knowingly.

"No," Bell lied.

His father waited patiently and raised an eyebrow.

Damn it. "Fine, he does, and I think it's cute," he admitted, not quite able to suppress a pout. It *was* cute, though. They were tiny, quiet little snores. Nice white noise to drift off to.

His dad laughed again. "Honeymoon stage, huh?"

Bell lifted one shoulder. "Maybe."

He clapped Bell on the shoulder and steered him back toward the kitchen. "Well, let me know when it starts keeping you up at night, and we'll schedule a consult."

Bell had learned through experience that it was easiest to just humor his father when he went into plastic-surgeon mode. "Sure thing, Dad."

"Are you planning on going back to the hospital today? We could go together."

He and Chris should talk about that. "Probably? I don't know for sure how long we're staying. Chris booked the tickets. I was sort of...." Bell waved a hand, embarrassed.

"I'm glad he stepped up. And you say he cooks? And makes coffee?" Bell's father clucked approvingly, and they stopped just short of the doorway to the kitchen, where they could see Chris pulling eggs and fruit out of the fridge.

It was nice to know Bell had one family member behind him, at least. He could still hardly believe his mother hadn't put up a bigger fuss. "Not exactly the boxes on Mom's list, but...."

Bell's father rolled his eyes. "Never mind about your mother's list. She'll come around. He seems to be doing pretty well by yours. And all that matters to me is that he seems to take pretty good care of you."

"Hey. I do my fair share of the looking after," Bell protested, thinking of the long hours Chris was prone to working—without eating—if Bell didn't intervene. "But thanks. I kind of think he's going to be around for a while, so...."

"Definitely remember what I said about the snoring, then."

CHAPTER THIRTEEN

BELL HAD just put the finishing touches on a last-minute Christmas promotion for the dance studio when the apartment door opened and Chris poked his head in. "Hey. You ready to go?"

Bell glanced at the clock. "You're early," he accused. He closed his laptop and set it to the side. He wasn't ready for their make-up date. "Is there a dress code?"

"Warm," Chris told him. When he stepped fully inside the apartment, Bell noted the knitted cap, gloves, scarf, and boots.

"Warm," he repeated. Did he even have all that gear? Most of what he had from his consultant days was designed for fashion, not functionality. "Got it."

He pulled on an extra sweatshirt, which barely fit under his coat, and a pair of smart gloves. On a hunch he checked the sleeve of his formal winter coat and came up with a cashmere scarf.

Well, at least it qualified as warm, though judging by the mismatched nature of Chris's accoutrements, he'd be overdressed. "I may need to go shopping," he confessed. When was the last time he'd spent any significant amount of time outside in the winter? Obviously he'd been far too concerned about the state of his hair back in his consultant days.

"I've got you covered for today." Chris held up a spare toque.

"Of course you do." Bell wrapped the scarf around his neck and then crossed the room to collect the hat and a kiss. "So, can you tell me where we're going now?"

"Nope." Chris smacked a kiss on Bell's cheek and then ushered him toward the shoe rack. "Still a surprise. Go get in the truck, okay? I have to grab a couple things from downstairs."

Bell took the keys and went to start the engine.

BABE IN THE WOODSHOP

It was already dark out and cold enough that he could see his breath. But the cheerful glow from Antonio's across the street and from the signs and holiday displays in the shop windows made the air feel warmer than it really was. For the first time in a long time, Bell found himself looking forward to Christmas.

A few minutes later, Chris joined him, hefted something into the bed of the truck, and climbed into the driver's seat. "Sorry for the delay. My mom called while I was packing things up."

"Triple confirming that you'll pick them up at the airport?"

"In fairness, their flight time changed, and this is the first time they've come back since my grandfather died. I didn't have room when I was living in the apartment, and the house has been a work in progress for a while."

That made sense. But Christmas was still a few weeks away. Back to the point at hand. "So. Packing things up?"

Chris rolled his eyes and put the truck in gear. "You're not very good at this being-surprised thing."

"We'll have to practice. Maybe I can do the surprising next time." All Bell knew about tonight was that it was to make up for the weekend to themselves they'd missed out on because of Cam's heart attack. Instead of spending Thursday at Will's, watching football and eating themselves stupid, they packed up a homemade turkey dinner in a dozen Tupperware containers, brought it to the hospital, and got on a plane home.

And then, of course, they'd spent the following week catching up on work instead of relaxing—Bell more so than Chris, since he had clients who needed holiday-promotion work. More than once he crawled into bed in the small hours of the morning and curled up against Chris's warmth, only to wake in the morning and find Chris already at work.

But the next thirty-six hours were just for the two of them.

"You're on," Chris agreed cheerfully as he signaled to turn down the street that would take them to his place.

Bell bit his lip in an effort not to ask, but once they'd gone past the house and then farther out toward true farm country, he couldn't keep quiet. "You sure you know where you're going?" he teased.

Chris stuck out his tongue. "I'm navigating by the stars," he shot back.

Bell was going to laugh, until Chris turned left into an empty field. "Well, you're certainly not navigating by road."

By then Chris had parked and turned off the engine. He smiled. "Come on."

Bell wasn't sure where they were supposed to be going, but he hopped out of the truck and followed Chris around to the back, where Chris was pulling off the tarp that covered the bed.

The bed that looked almost as cozy as a real bed, with pillows and sleeping bags and everything.

"Kinda chilly out here for alfresco sex," Bell said, mostly to cover how touched he was. People in movies went on stargazing dates in the backs of pickups. He'd never heard of anyone doing it in real life. And certainly no one had ever done anything this sweet for him.

"That can wait until spring," Chris agreed and dropped the tailgate, but he gave Bell a sly once-over anyway.

Bell reeled him in for a kiss and curled his gloves as best he could into the front of Chris's coat, until their lips touched. They both needed to use more lip balm. Chris's nose felt cold when it bumped his cheek.

Chris squeezed his butt when he pulled away, but not with the same sort of intent he'd had that morning before they got out of bed, so Bell figured that fighting frostbite wasn't on the to-do list. Though *he* still might be, when they got home—at least based on their recent track record.

"Come on, get in. It's cold out here."

Bell stepped up on the truck's bumper and climbed into the bed, trying not to get boot prints on the blankets. Chris came up after him and then sat down on the tailgate and pulled off his boots. Bell followed suit, but the winter air on his feet made him dive toward the opening of the sleeping bags.

The inside was warm—almost too warm. As Chris hauled over the cooler—that must've been what he put in the bed before they left the shop—Bell reached down toward his legs. His hand closed around a small, squishy, fabric-covered cushion. No. Not a cushion. It seemed to be filled with.... "Did you heat up a couple of Magic Bags before we left?"

Chris lifted a shoulder, shy but proud. "Well, you know. I didn't want you to get cold feet."

Bit late for that. Bell smiled and shifted over. "Get in here, come on. We are not spending all weekend in bed because you came down with something."

"Definitely not." He squeezed in next to Bell and then opened the lid of the cooler to reveal a giant Thermos, two travel mugs, a bag of mini marshmallows, and the aroma of hot chocolate. "How many marshmallows do you take in your cocoa?"

"Seven," Bell said seriously, just to see if Chris would really count them out. He did, adding the marshmallows to the bottom of the mug before pouring the hot chocolate. "Thanks."

Chris filled his own mug and then touched it against Bell's. His hot chocolate was good, but not as sweet as the kisses that preceded it. Or the ones Bell hoped would follow.

"So," he said, and he propped a few pillows behind them so they could lean back against the cab of the truck with Chris's arm around his shoulders. "This is a pretty good date. Though I have to tell you, you're going to make your life difficult if you keep raising the bar. I would've been happy with Netflix and takeout." Overhead, the stars burned brightly in an inky black sky. Bell couldn't remember the last time he'd taken a moment to appreciate a sight like that.

Chris shrugged, and the motion minutely jostled Bell's head as he rested it against Chris's chest. "I came up with the idea when I thought you were mad at me for avoiding you." He dropped a kiss on Bell's temple. "The original plan involved a meteor shower. For some reason I couldn't get the Leonids to reschedule."

Bell wanted to make light of it, but he couldn't find a joke, so he just gave Chris a squeeze around the middle and said, "We'll do it next year."

"It was cloudy that weekend anyway."

They sat like that, watching the stars traverse the sky, sipping their hot chocolate, until Bell's ass protested and his legs went tingly. He wiggled one leg to shake out the pins and needles.

"Time to get going?" Chris asked. He didn't sound disappointed.

"No, I just—" Bell grimaced and reached back to massage his buttcheek.

Oh. No wonder he was so uncomfortable. Ruefully he pulled his phone out of his back pocket and dropped it on top of the sleeping bag. "That's better."

Chris snorted. "No permanent damage, I hope?"

Bell picked it up and hit the button to light the screen. "No, it's fine," he said, noting that he had an e-mail notification.

"I didn't mean the phone."

Bell made a face at him and thumbed open the app through sheer muscle memory. He was about to turn it off and put it back—in a different pocket—but the e-mail subject line caught his attention and startled a laugh out of him. "Well, what do you know."

"Please tell me you're not going to be working tomorrow," Chris groaned theatrically.

Bell shook his head and held up the screen. "Nope," he said. Actually he was thinking about giving notice at Antonio's, but definitely not until after the holidays. He was starting to work too much again, and if Chris could cut back, so could he. "But I will be on Monday morning. Gonna have to make a stop at the post office."

Chris squinted but shook his head. "I don't have my glasses. What?"

Bell grinned. "Congratulations! We just sold our very first dildo."

ASHLYN KANE is a Canadian former expat who is now happy to be reunited with televised hockey at acceptable waking hours. She has reached the age of "twentysomething," which she will be for at least the next fifteen years.

She has a bad habit of staying up too late, a husband who likes to go to bed early, and a baby brother called Miracle Whip. She is allergic to cleaning, unless you mean cleaning up manuscripts, in which case she gets a little obsessive. Feel free to drop her a line—she's probably in front of her computer right now, since she's attached to it at the eyeballs.

Twitter: @ashlynkane
Facebook: www.facebook.com/ashlyn.kane.94

CLAUDIA MAYRANT has been exploring the world around her since she was old enough to get around under her own power. Her early travels took her on her bicycle "all the way to but not on the main road." Happily, since then, she's enjoyed visiting as many places as she can, from bustling marketplaces and enchanting castles to funky dives. She can't possibly decide which she likes best, but details of her favorite people, places, and things usually get put in the fiction blender so they can make an appearance in her stories.

Claudia maintains that each new adventure requires the appropriate footwear, which explains her closet. Her passion for taking photographs of the things she sees, does, and eats far exceeds her skill with the camera, but no matter the setting, she has fun trying to get a good shot.

For all her love of travel, she's most relaxed back in the South on a Gulf Coast beach with good friends, refreshing beverages, and plenty of sunscreen.

Her smartphone isn't literally connected to her hand, but anyone would be forgiven for thinking so.

Twitter: @claudiamayrant
Pinterest: ClaudiaMayrant

CJ BURKE's first book was the self-published *A Fancy Witch*, illustrated in crayon with particular attention to the witch's footwear. While CJ is now long past first grade, she's still hunting that perfect pair of equestrian boots.

CJ's life has always been centered on words. She's written a couple of those familiar yellow books about computers and more user guides for obscure software than necessary, but she's never given up the habit of plotting romances in her head during boring lectures or staff meetings. Along the way, she's been a lifeguard, an English professor, and a dozen other things in between. In a perfect world, CJ would work between an independent coffee shop and an amazing yarn & fabric store, then go home to alphabetize her spices while dancing around the kitchen to whatever's on the 80s channel.

CJ can be found on Ravelry, Instagram, and Twitter as cjburkebooks.

More from Ashlyn Kane

Ashlyn Kane
and Morgan James

HARD
FEELINGS

Rylan Williams hates conferences: too many people, not enough routine, and way too much interaction with strangers. When he gets stuck in a broken elevator with Miller Jones, the kid who fell asleep in his lecture, he figures things can't get worse. Then Rylan realizes he's the same guy he just spent an hour perving over from afar.

Rylan wants to await rescue in silence, but Miller insists on conversation, or at least banter. But just because they don't get along doesn't mean they don't have chemistry, and Rylan breaks all his rules about intimacy for a one-time-only conference hookup. He'll probably never see Miller again anyway. So of course, two months later Miller shows up at Rylan's office, having just been hired to work on a new computer program—with Rylan.

And Rylan thought being stuck in an elevator with him was bad.

Soon Rylan and Miller learn that they get along best when they take out their frustrations in the bedroom. Their arrangement goes against everything Rylan believes in, but the rules are simple: Don't stay overnight. Don't tell anyone. And don't fall in love.

This is probably a bad idea.

www.dreamspinnerpress.com

WINGING IT

ASHLYN KANE &
MORGAN JAMES

Gabe Martin has a simple life plan: get into the NHL and win the Stanley Cup. It doesn't include being the first out hockey player or, worse, getting involved with one of his teammates. But things change.

Dante Baltierra is Gabe's polar opposite—careless, reckless… shameless. But his dedication to the sport is impressive, and Gabe can overlook a lot of young-and-stupid in the name of great hockey. And Dante has a superlative ass in a sport filled with superlative asses.

Before Gabe can figure out how to deal, a tabloid throws him out of his comfortable closet into a brand-new world. Amid the emotional turmoil of invasive questions, nasty speculation, and on- and off-ice homophobia, his game suffers.

Surprisingly, it's Dante who drags him out of it—and then drags him into something else. Nothing good can come of secretly sleeping with a teammate, especially one Gabe has feelings for. But with their captain out with an injury, a rookie in perpetual need of a hug, and the race to make the playoffs for the first time since 1995, Gabe has a lot on his plate.

He can't be blamed for forgetting that nothing stays secret forever.

www.dreamspinnerpress.com

FOR **MORE** OF THE **BEST GAY** ROMANCE

Dreamspinner
PRESS
dreamspinnerpress.com

www.ingramcontent.com/pod-product-compliance
Lightning Source LLC
Chambersburg PA
CBHW060057260626

47160CB00005B/1697